A MAN OF FEW WORDS

Thelma Zirkelbach

A KISMET® Romance

METEOR PUBLISHING CORPORATION
Bensalem, Pennsylvania

To two superb speech pathologists: Kathryn Blakesley, my partner, with whom I've shared so much, and Peggy Engman, colleague, friend, and keeper of secrets.

And to Gayle Norstrom, friend and office manager, who keeps my life in order.

And special thanks to Carrie Lyons, early childhood teacher par excellence, for the cookie recipe.

THELMA ZIRKELBACH

When she isn't writing, Thelma Zirkelbach, who also writes as Lorna Michaels, is a speech pathologist who works with children. Sean Stuart is a compilation of many children whose lives and language she's shared. Grant Stuart, however, is a figment of her imagination, but since she's been happily married for over twenty years, it's just as well.

ONE

The moment Kelly Connery saw Sean Stuart she fell in love.

With a mop of blond curls, wide blue eyes, and chubby dimpled cheeks, he was one of the most appealing children she'd seen in her four years as staff speech pathologist at Cedar Grove Private School.

"He's adorable," she told her friend Marla Howard, who taught the three-year-old class in which Sean was enrolled.

Marla nodded. "But if you think the kid is cute," she said, rolling her eyes heavenward, "just wait until you meet the father. Six feet of gorgeous body, brown hair you want to run your fingers through, gray eyes deep enough to drown in, a voice that could haunt your dreams—"

"Okay, okay," Kelly said. "I get the picture. But you should be ashamed of yourself, ogling the parents of your preschoolers that way. If you weren't happily engaged, I'd worry about you. Besides, what would Mrs. Stuart think?"

"There is no Mrs. Stuart," Marla said.

"Divorced?"

Marla shook her head. "She died when Sean was two weeks old."

Kelly glanced across the room at Sean, who was absorbed in smearing both a sheet of paper and himself with blue fingerpaint. "Poor kid," she murmured. Her heart went out to any child who would miss a mother's love, especially this cherubic youngster with his impish smile.

"I'd like you to evaluate Sean's language," Marla said, interrupting Kelly's thoughts. "He started school a month ago, just after his third birthday. He's had time to adjust, but he hasn't said more than two words. At first I thought he was shy, but I spoke to the housekeeper and she said he doesn't talk at home either."

"Let me observe him for a few minutes," Kelly said. She made her way across the room, skirting toy trucks, blocks, and children, and sat beside Sean. "Hi."

The child looked up, cocked his head, and stuck his thumb in his mouth, dribbling blue paint down his chin.

Kelly extended a jar of red paint toward him. "Want some?"

The thumb left Sean's mouth and moved toward the paint. Kelly pushed the jar closer. He hesitated a moment, then dipped his finger in, took a moment to examine the fire engine red color, then broke into a grin. "Huh," he said and plunged his whole hand into the jar. Without a second's hesitation, Kelly picked up a jar of yellow paint and did the same.

In ten minutes she and Sean covered the paper with a rainbow of colors, but the child said nothing more than "huh."

She stood up, grimaced at the spot of yellow paint on her once-white sleeve, and strolled back to Marla. "I agree with you," she said. "Why don't you get Mr. Stuart's permission for me to do the assessment? I can see Sean Friday, and we can schedule a conference Monday to give Mr. Stuart the results."

Marla shook her head. "Better ask Pat to talk to him."

Kelly was surprised. "Why?" she asked. "You don't usually ask the principal to intercede for you."

"Not usually," Marla agreed. "But in this case—well, you'll see when you meet Grant Stuart."

Kelly knew that Pat Ferris's strongest asset was her ability to deal with the parents of her pupils. As principal of Cedar Grove, one of Houston's most exclusive private schools, Pat frequently had her work cut out for her. The school catered to money—old money gleaned from land and oil, new money from biotechnology and medicine. Along with wealth often came arrogance and excessive demands on school personnel. Kelly gave Marla a sympathetic smile. "Difficult parent, huh?"

"Yeah," Marla said. "Grant Stuart may be a hunk, but he isn't a friendly hunk. In fact, he can be downright hostile."

He was handsome, Kelly thought, as Grant Stuart sat down across from her at the conference table, but he didn't fit her definition of a hunk. His features were too classic, his manner too smooth. Hunks, in her estimation, were brawny and down-to-earth; this man, with his Brooks Brothers suit and his crisp white shirt, looked as if he'd gone straight from the Ivy League to the boardroom. Yet, when he'd shaken her hand just now, she'd been surprised to find his palm callused. A contradiction, she thought. A mystery. She'd always enjoyed mysteries.

Wanting to put him at ease while they waited for Marla and Pat, Kelly said, "I enjoyed testing Sean. He's a sweetheart."

"Thank you," Grant said and lapsed into silence.

Kelly gave him a reassuring smile. Perhaps he was nervous. Parents often were when they were about to receive the results of their child's evaluation or, for that matter, to have any type of conference at school. "Coffee, Mr. Stuart?" she inquired.

"Thanks. I'll get it," he said and walked over to the

credenza, poured himself a cup, and paused to look at the pictures of Cedar Grove students, from preschool through eighth grade, that covered the wall. When he returned to the table, he said, "Would you excuse me? I have some papers to go over."

Kelly nodded and watched him take a file from his briefcase, lean back in his chair, and become absorbed in reading.

While he studied his papers, Kelly studied him. If she'd met him in different circumstances, he'd be an interesting puzzle to solve—people always were. She decided she'd amuse herself by trying to fit a few of the pieces together.

He came from the South—Georgia perhaps, or Mississippi. She'd placed his accent the moment he'd told her good morning in a mellow baritone that flowed over her like a caress.

He was more than attractive. He was the kind of man a woman would kill for. His hair wasn't just brown but rich sable. His eyes weren't just gray but deep pewter, with a look that mesmerized.

Women must be standing in line for him, fascinated by his face and his physique, which was also memorable. They'd be drawn to his air of authority and intrigued by his distance. Who wouldn't want to bridge that chasm he seemed to put between himself and the world? She'd be jostling for a place in line herself if he weren't a client. But she knew better than to get involved with someone in the workplace. Educated by personal experience, she had developed an unswerving credo: never to mix her personal and professional lives. That could only spell disaster. So she would blot out Grant Stuart, the man, and concentrate on Mr. Stuart, the parent.

A sound from the doorway caught Kelly's attention, and she turned to see Pat Ferris enter the room, followed by Marla.

"Grant!" Pat said. "It's good to see you. I'm glad

you could come in this morning. You know Marla Howard, Sean's teacher, and I assume you've met Kelly Connery, our speech pathologist."

Grant Stuart inclined his head but said nothing. Goodness, the man had little more to say than his son. Kelly wondered if what Marla interpreted as hostility was simply Mr. Stuart's noncommunicative manner.

Pat sat down and turned to Marla. "Why don't you begin?"

Marla nodded. "Sean's a delightful little boy, but his communication skills are weak. He's friendly and outgoing, and he tries his best to make his needs known. But since he doesn't talk, he sometimes resorts to physical means—grabbing and hitting. I was concerned enough to call in our specialist." She gestured to Kelly.

"What did the language evaluation show?" Pat asked.

Kelly glanced at the folder she'd brought, then looked at Grant Stuart. He didn't lean forward or change his expression in any way; he simply stared at her with fathomless gray eyes.

She took a breath to suppress a mixture of nerves and annoyance and opened the folder. "My testing shows Sean has good understanding of what others say and he can perform nonverbal activities—matching, copying, remembering—quite well."

She paused. Still no reaction from Grant. Didn't he care about what she'd said? Was Sean just a possession to him like the Rolex on his wrist? No, he'd given permission for the testing, missed work to attend the conference. She glanced at his hand and saw that it was balled into a fist, the knuckles white. He cared all right. She felt a surge of sympathy.

She continued. "In spite of his other strong skills, Sean isn't using words to communicate. He gestures and makes sounds, but I heard no more than two or three words. How many words have you heard him use, Mr. Stuart?''

Grant frowned. "I don't know. Not many."

"Can you give me an estimate? Three? Ten? Twenty?''

He shrugged, looking uncertain. A flush stained his cheeks. "Three or four."

"That would put his language at about the fifteen-month level," Kelly said.

Instantly, Grant's eyes turned cold. The smoky gray of a moment ago was replaced by the frost of a winter morning. "Fifteen months. Are you suggesting the boy's retarded?" His voice was as icy as his eyes.

Kelly had dealt with this kind of reaction before, so she answered easily, "Of course not. As I said, his other skills are normal. Only his ability to express himself is weak. He isn't retarded, but he does have an expressive language delay.''

"I see," Grant said. "What's the cause?"

"We can't be sure. Often we can't pinpoint a specific reason for language problems. But we do know how to treat them; that's the important thing." She glanced back at her papers. "When did he say his first word, Mr. Stuart?''

Again Grant Stuart looked uncomfortable. "I'm not sure. You'd have to ask the housekeeper. She'd know better than I.''

The sympathy Kelly had felt a moment ago faded, replaced by anger. The man seemed to know very little about his son. She'd bet her professional license he never talked to the child. Poor Sean. No mother and an uncommunicative father. She looked up from the folder as Grant said to Pat, "We've established that the boy doesn't talk. We've established that Ms. Connery doesn't know why. What do you propose to do about it?''

Pat smiled reassuringly. "I'm sure Ms. Connery has some suggestions.''

Did she ever! "Yes, I do. I'll be brief," Kelly added, noting Grant's quick glance at his watch. "I'd like to work with Sean at school, do some language stimulation, see if we can get him started talking."

"For how long?"

"Thirty-minute sessions. I'd prefer seeing him daily, but three times a week would be acceptable."

"What I meant, Ms. Connery, is how long your treatment will go on."

"I can't give you an exact timetable," Kelly replied. She heard this question from many parents. "There are many factors involved and—"

"A month," Grant said.

"I beg your pardon?"

"A trial period. Show me some progress in a month, and then I'll decide whether the boy should continue with you."

"Mr. Stuart, there are no guarantees in this kind of treatment. I can't—"

"One month, Ms. Connery." He stood up.

Kelly stared up at the impassive face, the cool gray eyes. She was tempted to tell Mr. Stuart what he could do with his month, but she thought of Sean and couldn't. The child needed her. Besides, she'd never been one to back away from a challenge. She nodded. "A month, Mr. Stuart."

"And see him every day."

Kelly suppressed a smile. "All right. I'll begin tomorrow."

Parent participation was an important part of language treatment, and as soon as she began working with Sean, Kelly promised herself she'd do everything possible to get Grant Stuart involved. *He'd* be a challenge, too.

She gathered her papers and followed Marla to the door. As she passed Grant and Pat, she heard the principal's quiet voice. "I know it hasn't been easy, Grant, raising Sean alone."

At the words, Kelly saw an expression of such raw pain cross Grant Stuart's face that she felt it like a blow to her midsection. As she walked down the hall with Marla, Kelly said, "He's had a rough time."

"Who? Grant or Sean?"

"Grant. Didn't you see the way he looked at Pat just then? He's still grieving over his wife."

"Maybe. But Sean's my concern. Grant Stuart's a big boy. He can take care of himself." Marla entered the teachers' lounge and flopped down on the couch. "He's a cold fish," she said.

Kelly sat beside her. Still musing over Grant's pained expression, she said, "Maybe he's not as cold as he acts."

"No? What's he like then?"

"Mysterious."

Marla laughed. "Kelly Connery, ever the romantic. Well, I think he's just cold. Why else would he refer to Sean as 'the boy'? Not once did he refer to his son by name. If that isn't cold, I don't know what is."

Kelly had no answer to that or to anything else that had happened this morning: Grant Stuart's attitude toward Sean, her own reactions to Grant—that first spark of attraction, the simmering anger when he'd seemed so unaware of his child, and then the rush of sympathy she'd felt at the anguish in his eyes.

Pushing her mixed emotions aside, she addressed Marla's comment. "Maybe his feelings will change when Sean starts to talk. Some parents can't relate to kids who don't say anything. Getting him involved in Sean's treatment might help. I'll call him in a week or so and have him observe one of our sessions."

Marla grimaced. "If you expect Grant Stuart to cooperate, I'd say you have your work cut out for you."

Grant turned the key in the ignition, and the Mercedes purred to life. Yet even though he was an hour behind schedule, he let the car idle. The conference had shaken him, and although he wanted to put the last hour out of his mind, he couldn't. He'd expected the morning to play havoc with his emotions. Though he'd prepared himself, shielded himself with silence and indifference, tension still made his stomach churn and his hands sweat. Pain he'd tried to avoid, guilt he'd tried to suppress, assailed him. Taking a deep breath, he struggled to bury his feelings.

He stepped on the accelerator and headed for downtown Houston. With his eyes on the traffic, he slid one hand over and opened his briefcase, then felt inside for the small tape recorder he always carried. He pressed the record button and began to dictate.

"Memo: Call Matt Faber at Shields and Barnett and see how they're coming on landscaping plans for the Boston project. Tell them I want to see preliminary sketches ASAP.

"Memo: Make a note in Sean's personal file. He begins speech therapy on three fifteen. School will bill for the sessions."

He flipped off the machine and put it aside and again wished he could turn off his emotions as easily. But he wasn't a machine, dammit, and although he could generally ignore his feelings, whenever he was confronted with Sean, they resurfaced.

Once more his thoughts focused on the conference he'd attended, and he picked up the recorder again. "Report of language evaluation should arrive by next Wednesday. If not, call school and check with Ms. Connery."

He'd liked Ms. Connery. She seemed warm, and goodness knew, Sean needed some warmth in his life. He hoped she was as competent as Pat Ferris had assured him.

Ms. Connery had been disgusted when he admitted he didn't know when Sean began talking. He wasn't about to explain that Sean's first year or so was a pain-filled blur in his memory. Let Ms. Connery think what she liked . . . and he had a good idea what her thoughts were. Just for a moment, when he'd stood up, she'd looked as though she wanted to take a punch at him. Though she'd quickly masked the fury, there'd been an instant when her eyes had flashed fire.

Green. Her eyes were green. He wondered why he should have noticed the color or remembered it but, unaccountably, he did. In fact, he had a very clear picture of Kelly Connery in his mind. Eyes the clear green of a mountain stream. Strawberry-blond hair that curled riotously around her face. A turned up nose and a mouth that seemed designed for smiling.

His thoughts turned to another woman, and he wondered, with annoyance, why he seemed to compare every female he met, under whatever circumstances, to his late wife. Kelly Connery fell in the not-like-Claudia category. No, she was not like Claudia at all. She reminded him of a sprite or perhaps a water nymph.

God, what was he doing, waxing poetic about someone he'd spent only thirty minutes with? The important thing was that Kelly Connery be good for Sean. Because *he* didn't have time to be. Quieting the voice inside that said there were more barriers between him and Sean than lack of time, he turned onto the freeway and made a futile effort to put both Sean and Kelly Connery out of his mind.

The next morning, Kelly glanced at the clock on the wall of the school speech clinic. Eight forty-five. Her first session with Sean Stuart was at nine, but she'd wait a few extra minutes. On rainy mornings like this, children often arrived at school late. She glanced out her window and saw a long line of automobiles snaking across the parking lot. Children in shiny raincoats, arms loaded with books and lunch boxes, emerged from cars and sloshed through puddles toward the school entrance. Several teachers huddled under umbrellas, directing traffic. Kelly felt a twinge of sympathy. *What a day for carpool duty.*

She'd had enough of the elements just getting out of her own car. Now she was happy to be snug and dry in her room, she decided, turning to survey her domain. As usual, she felt a sense of pleasure. The room was small but serviceable and, thanks to posters of Sesame Street characters and artwork by her students, was warm and welcoming as well. Of course, she'd like more storage space, and the cabinets should be brightly colored instead of white—

Someday, she told herself. Someday, when she had her own school, she'd have everything just the way she wanted. And someday was fast approaching. Two years at most and she'd have the money. A year if she were lucky and made enough at her summer job. Then her dream of a preschool for children with language disorders would be a reality.

She checked her watch again. Time for Sean. As always, she felt a sense of anticipation when she started a new student. She loved working with little ones, hearing their first words, and knowing she could give them the gift of language.

She hurried to Marla's room and opened the door to find Marla, her aide, and twelve three-year-olds seated in a circle on the carpet, their attention focused on a large calendar. "What's the weather today?" Marla asked. "Can anyone tell me?"

"Rain," came a chorus of childish voices.

"Lotta rain," added one ponytailed pixie.

"You're right," Marla told her. "Come up here, Stephanie, and put the rain picture on today's date." When Stephanie had finished, Marla turned to Sean. "Sean, Miss Kelly's here to see you. She's going to take you to play some more games."

The child gave Kelly a dimpled grin and trotted over to her.

"Hi," Kelly said.

Sean said nothing but gave her another smile. He put a chubby hand in hers, and she led him down the hall.

Once in her own room, Kelly gave Sean a few minutes to look around. His eyes lit on a three-dimensional figure of Big Bird. He fingered the yellow crepe-paper feathers. "Huh," he said.

"Bird," Kelly said.

"Huh?"

"Big Bird. On TV."

"Um," the child replied.

When he finished inspecting the picture, Kelly reached for a jar of soap bubbles. "Sean, look! Bubbles! Let's open it. Here." She held it out. "Open."

Sean removed the top and peered into the jar. "Bubbles," Kelly whispered. "Look." She blew through the plastic ring, and a myriad of rainbow-colored bubbles swirled around them. "Pop!" she cried and proceeded to pop the ones she could reach. Crowing with delight, Sean followed suit as Kelly called, "Pop, pop." When the bubbles disappeared, she said, "All gone."

"Ah ah," Sean mimicked her tone.

"Yes, all gone. Want more?"

"Huh."

Again and again, they blew bubbles. Again and again, they popped them. Again and again, Kelly cried, "Pop!" At last she was rewarded with a "Puh" from Sean. "Good boy!" she cried.

After several other activities, she took Sean back to his classroom. "Bye," she told him.

"Bye," he responded, using one word of his three-word vocabulary.

Kelly winked at Marla. "Success," she said. "I'll have some progress for Mr. Stuart by the end of a month. Bet on it."

Early the following Monday Kelly wandered into the teachers' lounge, where several of her colleagues lingered over coffee before heading for their classrooms.

She felt tired and achy. Maybe some coffee would get her going. She poured herself a cup and wrinkled her nose as she tasted. "Ugh. How long has this been brewing?"

"Almost as long as it's been raining out," someone answered.

"You know the worst thing about this rain?" said Joan Heller, the fourth-grade teacher. "It makes your hair frizz. Saturday night at the Ashtons' party I felt like a frump."

"Speaking of frumps, did you see Mindy Carlton?" another of the teachers inquired. "She looked like—"

Kelly tuned out the conversation. The school gossip mill was in session. That was the one thing she didn't like about Cedar Grove. The school was like a small town where everyone knew everyone else's business. The teachers came from the same social class as the parents and mingled with them at parties, fund-raisers, church. The parents approved, feeling the staff "understood" their children. While that might be true, such close association also generated gossip. Kelly didn't mingle, and she didn't gossip. She kept her private life private, her eyes fastened on her goals.

"What about you, Kelly?" Cathy Turner, who'd just replaced a teacher on maternity leave, asked. "Going to the Harrisons' tomorrow?"

Kelly shook her head. She had no idea what was going on tomorrow night. Her Tuesday evenings were spent in an accounting class, preparing for the school she planned.

Now Joan Heller remarked, "I hear you're working with Grant Stuart's son. He's a nice man, very personable."

That got Kelly's attention. Joan's description of Grant was the exact opposite of Marla's and of Kelly's own impression. Suddenly, she was very interested in the conversation.

"We used to run into him and his wife at parties,"

Joan went on. "Since she died though, we haven't seen much of him. Not many singles in our crowd, and from what I hear, Grant doesn't stick to any one woman. Just plays the field. And works."

"He's in real estate, isn't he?" Kelly asked. "I seem to remember that from the school records."

"Yeah, real estate with a capital *R*. He develops shopping malls all over the country."

Cathy turned toward Kelly. "You're single, he's single. Maybe you can interest him in developing something with you."

Kelly stiffened, but she kept her answer light. "Not a chance. My only interest in Grant Stuart is professional."

"Maybe you should rethink your policies, hon. Grant's a mighty attractive man," Joan said. "In fact, he's A-one gorgeous."

"Sure, no harm in adding a little pleasure to your business," Cathy agreed with a lazy smile.

That had crossed her mind, Kelly thought guiltily. In fact, she'd been thinking about the enigmatic Grant Stuart much too often. A blush rose to her cheeks. Hoping her colleagues didn't notice, she said, "Nope. The Connery First Commandment is 'Thou shalt not mix work and play.' " She laughed as Joan and Cathy groaned in unison. Then she picked up her raincoat and purse. "I need some paper from the supply room. See you all later."

"I'll come along," Marla offered.

As they walked, Kelly turned to her friend. "Can you imagine how tongues would wag if I got involved with a parent?"

"Maybe not. Grant *is* single. And, as Joan says, he *is* A-one gorgeous, but—"

"But what?" she asked as they went into the supply room.

"He's great to look at, but I wouldn't want to touch."

Kelly began selecting various colors of construction paper. "I still think he's just quiet."

"Okay, he's somber and silent. By the way, how are you coming along with your plan to get him involved in treatment?"

Kelly sighed. "Not well. I've left three messages—"

"I told you. Grant's a tough one."

"Well, so am I," Kelly said. "I'll find a way if I have to drag him in by his designer lapels. In fact, I think I'll give him another call now."

She headed for the door, but as she passed a window, she glanced out. A silver Mercedes moved into the carpool line. Kelly squinted to see through the driving rain. "Better yet, I'll talk to him in person. He just drove up."

"Kelly, you can't go out in this rain," Marla objected.

"Of course I can," Kelly said, trying unsuccessfully to stifle a sneeze.

"You sound like you're coming down with something," Marla pointed out. "The last thing you need is to get wet."

"Won't hurt me a bit." Kelly dumped her construction paper into Marla's arms and pulled on her raincoat. "Stand back, Marla. Grant Stuart is about to get a dose of the Connery charm."

"Charm?" Marla raised a brow.

Kelly grinned. "Translation: he's about to get bulldozed." With a wave over her shoulder, she marched out of the room.

TWO

Grant edged the car a little farther toward the school entrance, then reached for the *Wall Street Journal* he'd laid beside him. He scanned the paper for articles on real estate, found one that interested him, and settled back to read. He was engrossed in the article when a knock on the passenger-side window caught his attention. Startled, he looked up. Kelly Connery stood outside the car, rain beating down on her, saying something he couldn't make out. Good Lord, she was getting soaked. He leaned across the seat and opened the door. "Get in."

Bringing a torrent of rainwater with her, she slid into the car. She looked like a bedraggled puppy as she sat dripping all over his leather upholstery. She took a swipe at her hair and managed to splatter the dashboard and console as well.

Sean, delighted by Kelly's arrival, leaned forward in his car seat and made welcoming sounds. She grinned. "Hi, Sean."

His defenses firmly in place, Grant frowned at her. "What are you doing here? This isn't the weather for socializing."

"This isn't a social call, Mr. Stuart," she replied. "I've been trying to reach you."

"So I noticed. I've had three messages." When he'd gotten the first one, he'd felt a surge of pleasure at seeing her name. For all of thirty seconds he'd indulged himself in the absurd fantasy that she was making a play for him. But he knew better.

"I wanted to talk to you about Sean," she said, confirming what he'd already surmised.

She sat, no doubt waiting for an apology or a polite excuse for not returning her calls. He wasn't inclined to give her either. He didn't care to manufacture a lie, or to admit the real reason—that he couldn't bear to dredge up the uncomfortable feelings that a discussion of Sean would precipitate. Dammit, he didn't owe her an explanation. "I've been busy," he said.

Her eyes flashed—the same green fire he remembered from their last meeting—but she responded in a placate-the-parent tone. "I'm sure you have, but I really would like to get together with you. Parent participation is important in language treatment. I'd like you to observe one of Sean's sessions."

Grant regarded her warily. "You came out in a cloudburst to tell me that?"

"Telephoning didn't seem to work," she said and grinned. She had a tiny space between her front teeth and a light dusting of freckles across her nose. As he nudged the car forward, he was almost sorry they were nearly at the building entrance. Despite her reason for approaching him, his annoyance had faded and he realized he'd enjoy talking with her a while longer. He prolonged the conversation by changing the subject. "I hope you have an extra pair of shoes stashed in your therapy room." He let his gaze travel from the top of her sodden head down to her shoes, which were leaving puddles on the floor. "You'll have to admit, you are a bit—" He wanted to say "waterlogged" but he settled for "damp." His lips twitched.

She lifted her chin defiantly, then spoiled the effect by sneezing.

"God bless you," he said and watched her fumble in the pocket of her raincoat and come up empty-handed. "Tissue?" he offered, reaching in his coat for a packet.

"Thanks."

"Take several. Looks like you're going to need them."

"I doubt it. I never catch cold," she retorted and sneezed again. She muttered something under her breath, then shrugged and smiled sheepishly. "You still haven't answered my question," she said, serious again. "When can you come by and watch me work with Sean?"

"I'm leaving town today. I'll be gone several weeks."

"When you come back then?"

God, she was persistent, but he hit upon an answer he hoped would cut her off. "Ms. Connery, I'm paying *you* to work with the boy. If I had the time or expertise, I'd work with him myself."

"But—"

"If you want someone to observe your session, get in touch with Olivia, my housekeeper. She spends more time with Sean than I do."

"I'll do that, but I'd still like you to come," she insisted.

She wasn't going to give up, Grant realized. He felt a sudden desire to see this firebrand again, but equally strong was his aversion to unpleasant emotions. Avoidance won, for the moment. "You're still on trial, Ms. Connery," he said. "A month, remember?"

"Oh, I'll pass the test," she said. As Grant pulled up to the school entrance, she opened the door. "You can expect a call when you're back in town. See you then. Bye, Sean." She got out of the car and shut the door.

As he unbuckled Sean's seat belt and handed him out of the car to a waiting teacher, Grant watched Kelly walk back inside, waving to several youngsters she passed.

By the time he'd pulled out of the parking lot, he'd begun to laugh. A deep, full-bodied laugh such as he hadn't experienced in over three years. He'd been right. Kelly Connery was a gutsy lady. He thought of how she'd looked, rainwater dripping from her hair, and remembered he'd likened her to a water nymph the other day.

She intrigued him. And because of that, she was dangerous. But he'd always been a risk taker in business. Why not in his personal life as well? The thought of getting to know Ms. Connery . . . personally . . . appealed to him.

Besides, she was right. He should be aware of what happened in Sean's therapy program, no matter how painful that might prove. Okay, maybe he was a fool, but when he got back to Houston, he'd pay Kelly Connery the visit she'd requested.

That evening Kelly curled up on her couch, a cup of tea in her hand and a box of tissues on the table beside her. "And the worst of it, Walter, was that I accomplished nothing with Grant Stuart. Zip! Zero!" She sniffled. "I even ruined a brand new pair of Amalfi loafers."

The large gray tomcat in the armchair blinked at her disinterestedly. Walter seldom paid attention to conversation unless it included the words *kitty food*.

Nevertheless, Kelly continued. "You'd think he'd take time for his only son—all he has left from his marriage." She sniffled again and reached for another tissue. "Why are all the most attractive men such cold fish? Yes, that includes you, Walter," she added, punctuating her sentence with a sneeze.

Walter opened one eye. Kelly walked over to his chair and scooped him up. Affronted, he squirmed in her arms.

"Oh, no, after the salmon I gave you this morning, the least you can do is cheer me up. Cuddling won't compromise your dignity." She sat back on the couch, settled Walter in her lap, and began to stroke him. Apparently he decided to humor her, for he snuggled against her and purred.

As she petted the cat, Kelly replayed the conversation with Grant Stuart in her mind. He'd been cold, almost angry; yet something drew her to him. Not just his handsome face; it was the haunted look in his eyes that drew her and the hint of vulnerability behind the arrogance. Despite their conflict, those moments in his car—the musky scent of his cologne mingling with the smell of leather, the deep, musical timbre of his voice, the curtain of rain that isolated them—seemed oddly intimate.

What was she thinking? She knew better than to let a lazy Southern drawl and a pair of stormy gray eyes make her heart beat faster. She didn't—*didn't*, she repeated to herself—have an ulterior motive in wanting Mr. Stuart to visit her therapy room. This was business.

And if, by some small chance, she *did* want to see him again for personal reasons, she'd squelch that. Right now. Because Nick had taught her all she needed to know about the perils of letting the personal interfere with the professional. And she wasn't a slow learner. She needed only one lesson.

Walter's steady purring had a calming effect. Kelly decided not to dwell on past hurts. She'd think about the present. No good, she amended, stifling yet another sneeze. The immediate present offered nothing better than a head cold. The future then. First step: get in touch with Grant Stuart's housekeeper. Setting Walter down, she reached for the telephone directory.

Olivia Stillwell was a pleasant surprise, Kelly thought, glancing at the woman she'd met just minutes before. A plump sixtyish lady with gray hair, calm blue eyes, and a ready smile, Olivia looked like someone you'd love to have as a grandmother. And she clearly adored Sean.

"Sean's my second-generation Stuart," she told Kelly as they walked down the hall with the child between them. "I came to work for the Stuarts thirty-five years ago, when Grant was two months old. Now there was a handful, let me tell you. Anyway, I raised Grant and his brother and sister, and then a few years ago, I retired.

"When Claudia got pregnant, Grant asked me to come for a month and help her take care of the baby. I don't think Claudia was too happy—she wanted an English nanny—but Grant said, 'It's Olivia or nobody!' Well, my own kids were grown, and Albert—he was my husband for thirty years—had died, and I had nothing to keep me in Atlanta, so when Sean was born, I packed my bags and came to Houston.

"Then two weeks later, the terrible accident happened and the poor little tyke was left without a mother. So I told Grant, 'I'm here as long as you need me.' And he hasn't sent me home yet," she finished with a broad smile.

"He's lucky to have you," Kelly said. "You must be very fond of Sean. And Grant."

"Love them both like they were my own," Olivia said.

By now they'd reached Kelly's room. Inside, Olivia eased her ample body into one of the small chairs. "You know, I've been worried about Sean for a long time. Seemed like he should have been talking much earlier. I mentioned that to Grant several times, but—" She cleared her throat and changed the subject. "I'm glad you're working with Sean. Now, if you'll just show me some things I can do, well, I'll help all I can."

"Great!" Kelly encouraged Olivia to watch the way she interacted with Sean, then wrote down a dozen words to work on at home and suggested they get back together in a week. Kelly felt this woman had an intuitive understanding of how to help Sean. She wished she could say the same for the child's father.

A thought came to her as she began putting materials away. "I'd like to make a scrapbook for Sean. It's a great tool for getting children to talk. I'll need a picture of Sean, one of you, and one of his father. Can you get those to me?"

"They'll be here tomorrow." Olivia got up and shook Kelly's hand. "Thank you for asking me to come today. I can see you're going to be good for my little fellow."

"Thanks," Kelly said. She took Sean back to his room, feeling pleased with herself. The scrapbook was a good idea. She'd used it with other youngsters, but with Sean she had a special purpose in mind. She'd inundate him with pictures of his father. By the time Grant Stuart returned to Houston, she'd have Sean saying "Daddy"; and if that didn't get Grant involved in Sean's therapy, she didn't know what would.

The next morning as Kelly crossed the parking lot she saw Olivia leaning out the window of a small blue Honda. "I brought the pictures," Olivia called, waving a manila envelope.

In her room Kelly opened the envelope and drew out three snapshots. The first showed Sean sitting on his Big Wheel. The second was a shot of Olivia holding up a box wrapped in Christmas paper. But the third picture, the one of Grant Stuart, drew Kelly's attention.

This was a different Grant Stuart from the cool, suspicious man she'd met in the last few weeks. He stood by a wooden fence, wearing jeans, boots, and a western shirt, his hair ruffled by the wind. But the clothing, although far removed from what she'd seen him wearing, wasn't the major difference. The photo couldn't have been more than a few years old, but this Grant

Stuart was a lifetime younger. He laughed into the camera, his expression vibrant and carefree.

Looking at the picture, Kelly felt an intense desire to take his hand, to laugh with him, to face the world with the same confidence and bravado. What had happened to this Grant Stuart? What had changed him into the sardonic man she'd talked to a few days ago? She remembered the look of anguish she'd seen when he'd spoken to the principal after their conference. A tragedy, yes. He'd lost his wife. But there had to be more than that . . . something to make him so distant with his son and so wary of the world. Grant Stuart was a man with secrets.

She smoothed her hand across the photograph and put it back in the envelope. Then she headed for the teachers' workroom, where she made several photocopies of the pictures.

During Sean's session, Kelly began the scrapbook. In Marla's room, she tacked a copy of Grant's pictures in Sean's locker. "Point out the pictures every time Sean goes to his locker," Kelly told Marla, "and encourage him to say 'Daddy.' "

"Ah," Marla said. "Do I detect a method of getting 'Daddy' involved?"

"You do. I'm willing to try anything."

Kelly went back to her room, hung a picture of Grant on her bulletin board, and put another in the box of materials she planned to use with Sean the next day. By the time she'd finished, she'd used up all the pictures of Grant but one. She was tempted to take the remaining copy home, but that wasn't necessary. She could see him in her mind—young and happy, his gray eyes alight with laughter. The picture evoked tender feelings. She wanted to brush that errant lock of hair back from his brow, to—

Stop, she told herself. *You're not going to let a picture haunt you.* But she knew it would.

A week later, Kelly grinned at Marla. "My plan's

working.'' Every time they'd come upon a picture of
Grant, she had pointed it out with much excitement.
Soon Sean began imitating ''Daddy,'' and finally he'd
started saying the word on his own. She only hoped,
Kelly thought wryly, that Sean would recognize the
somber, real-life Grant Stuart as the same man in the
picture.

She'd just come out of Marla's room when the school
secretary stopped her. ''Kelly, phone call on line two.''

Kelly hurried into the office and picked up the exten-
sion phone. ''Kelly Connery,'' she said.

''Ms. Connery,'' said a rich, masculine voice. ''This
is Grant Stuart.''

He didn't have to identify himself. Kelly recognized
his voice immediately. ''Yes, Mr. Stuart.''

''You sound surprised to hear from me.''

''I am,'' she admitted.

''You said you wanted to get together.'' His voice
was seductive, the honeyed tones of the South coming
through more clearly on the phone. They made his
words sound as though he referred to a moonlight tryst.

Kelly cleared her throat and tried to sound businesslike. ''Ah . . . yes. When would you like to come in?''

''How about tomorrow?'' he asked. ''I'm taking an
early flight into Hobby Airport. I could swing by the
school before I go to my office.''

''Wonderful. I'll see you then.'' Kelly hung up the
phone and grinned. The elusive Mr. Stuart had called.
Now, if Sean would oblige her by saying ''Daddy,''
she was certain she'd be able to get his father involved
in therapy. Surely as soon as he heard his son speak to
him, Grant Stuart would be hooked.

THREE

The next morning Kelly took Sean to her room early and got out a puzzle for him to work on while they waited for his father.

She was nervous, Kelly realized. Grant Stuart was disconcerting. Perhaps the notable difference between the photograph and the man bothered her. Or perhaps it was his commanding presence. At any rate, she didn't feel her customary confidence in meeting a parent.

When she heard the knock on her door, she felt another flutter of nerves but made herself get up calmly and open it.

How could she have forgotten how tall he was? Tall and lean and . . . gorgeous, she thought looking up past curving lips and a Roman nose into gray eyes that now seemed the color of wood smoke. He must have driven from the airport with the windows open, for he smelled of fresh air along with tangy after-shave and some indefinable element that she recognized as quint-essentially male.

She hoped her voice wouldn't sound breathless when she said good morning. She was spared, however, by Sean, who looked up from the puzzle and spotted his father. With a cry of delight, he leaped out of his chair, ran across the room, and threw his arms around Grant's legs. "Da-ee!" he shouted. "Daddy."

Kelly saw surprise in Grant's eyes, followed by pain. Then, as if he were drawing a curtain, he seemed to turn off his emotions and register nothing at all. He hesitated, hand poised in mid-air, then reached down awkwardly to pat the child's head.

Sean, hugging his father's legs, was unaware of Grant's reactions, but Kelly wasn't. She felt a mixture of pain and disappointment. Loving a child was so easy. Why did this man seem to lack that capacity? To hide her feelings, she said quietly, "Sean, let Daddy come in."

Instead, Sean lifted his arms to his father and said, "Up!"

Grant was in control now, Kelly saw. Without expression, he lifted the child and carried him over to a small chair.

Grant turned to Kelly. "I see you've made progress."

"Four new words—*up, daddy, more,* and *allgone.*" She tried, unsuccessfully, to keep the pride in Sean out of her voice.

Grant's brow shot up. "Only four words in four weeks."

"The first words always take a long time," Kelly said, irritated at his attitude but keeping her voice calm. After all, she reminded herself, she knew what she was talking about. "Later the words will snowball."

"Mmm," Grant said.

Pompous, thought Kelly. *Gorgeous, but pompous.* "It's a better average than three words in three years."

Grant's lips curved. "Touché, Ms. Connery." Then he said in a businesslike tone, "I'm here to observe your session. What would you like me to do?"

"Join in, Mr. Stuart. This is hands-on. Come on, Sean," she said, sitting down on a brightly colored rug and patting the place beside her. "Let's play." She reached behind her for a box labeled "Mr. Potato Head."

Sean joined her on the rug, then turned to Grant. "Da-ee?"

"Yes, Daddy, too." Kelly motioned to a spot beside Sean and was gratified to see that, although he grimaced, Grant complied. He sat on the rug as if expecting it to bite him and adjusted the crease in his trousers. Was this the first time he'd sat on the floor to play with Sean? The other Grant Stuart, the one in the photograph, looked as if he would enjoy romping with a small child, but this man was totally out of his element.

Loosen up, Kelly wanted to order him, but instead she said, "Language therapy works best in a group. Since I don't have an appropriate group for Sean at school, you'll be our group today."

Grant tried his best, she could see. He sat gamely through Mr. Potato Head and bubble popping and even accepted a snack of juice and goldfish crackers. But he just wasn't comfortable seated on the floor interacting with a child. *Okay, Kelly. You have your work cut out for you.* "I'm going to take Sean back to his room a few minutes early so we can talk," she said, getting up. "Sean, tell Daddy bye."

When she left him, Grant stared absently at the colorful bulletin board, then frowned and walked closer. *What the hell?* Here was his picture—an old one at that—tacked up on the wall. Where had it come from? For a moment he gazed at the photo, bemused, thinking back to an earlier time in his life, a time before heartache and betrayal.

When the door opened, he started. Kelly stood in the doorway. "I asked Olivia for pictures of the family," she said. "I made copies of yours and put it everywhere, so whenever Sean saw you we could practice saying 'Daddy.' We made a scrapbook, too. Would you like to see it?"

"All right."

"Be right back."

Grant sat down gingerly in one of the chairs by the low rectangular table. His knees were table height, and the back of the chair barely came up to his waist. He twisted uncomfortably.

Kelly appeared from behind a bookshelf and stood looking at him. He could see she was doing her best not to laugh.

"Feeling out of place?" she inquired. "I'll take pity on you. Come in my office, and you can have a grown-up chair."

He got up and followed her. He felt more than a bit out of place, surrounded by all the paraphernalia of childhood. Kelly opened a door at the back of the room and motioned him into a cubbyhole with a desk, two chairs—both adult size, thank God—and a crowded bookshelf. She opened the scrapbook, and Grant tried to sound properly enthusiastic about its contents.

When they'd finished with it, she said, "Sean's made gains."

"Yes, he has," Grant agreed, "and I can see you get along well with him." He spread his hands. "What can I say, Ms. Connery? You've convinced me. Go ahead and work with him as long as you need to."

Her eyes lit up. "I hoped you'd say that. He's such a delightful child, with great potential. I'm enjoying him."

She meant it. Or else she was a good actress. Perhaps the latter was true. Could a grown woman enjoy spending her time with three-year-olds and Mr. Potato Head? Well, that wasn't his problem. He gave her a nod and said, "That's all settled then. Just continue as you have—"

She put up her hand. "I will, but I need your help."

He frowned. "What do you mean?"

"I see Sean for half an hour a day. Think of all

the hours I *don't* see him. He needs constant language stimulation.''

"He's getting that at school.''

"But he needs it at home, too.''

Grant sighed. "Haven't you talked with Olivia?''

"Yes, she's a gem. She's been in twice and she's working beautifully with Sean. But you need to be involved, too.''

"Ms. Connery, I told you before, I'm a busy man.'' He could feel her disapproval, but dammit, what he'd said was true. He was too busy to sit on the floor and pop bubbles. *And too scared*, added a little voice inside him, a voice he forced himself to ignore. "Besides,'' he added. "I'm not trained to do this . . . this kind of work.''

Cynically, he waited for her response. At this point, most women he knew would offer to provide a little private training.

Instead, Kelly laughed without a trace of guile. "You don't need training.''

Grant felt both relieved and disappointed at her response. The thought of some private moments with Ms. Connery wasn't at all unpleasant. He listened as she continued.

"Just talk to Sean. Talk to him when he's in the bathtub—''

"He's had his bath when I get home.''

"Take him to the grocery store.''

"I don't do the grocery shopping.''

"Take him fishing.'' She hesitated a moment as if weighing her words, then went on. "Sean's not going to go away, Mr. Stuart. He's going to be around for a long time.''

Her words hit home. The wound was sharp and deep, but that was something he'd deal with later, in private. Now, he masked his emotions and, to distract himself, focused on Kelly Connery's face. "Your point is well taken. Where should I start?''

"Why don't you take him somewhere—just the two of you?"

"Where?" With surprise and guilt, he realized he'd never taken Sean places and hadn't the faintest notion where a three-year-old might want to go. "An Astros game?" he suggested.

Kelly laughed, showing just a trace of dimple in her right cheek. "I doubt he's into baseball. Why don't you try the zoo? Do you like elephants?" she added, straight-faced.

"Not much," he muttered. "Besides, I—"

"I know. You're a busy man, but you must take a day off sometime. How about a few hours on Saturday afternoon?"

She had a sweet voice. Even when she lectured him, the sound was appealing. "I'll be out of town Saturday," he said. "I'm going back to Boston day after tomorrow."

"Surely you'll be back."

Her skin looked milky soft. He wondered if it felt as satiny as it looked. "I'll be back next Friday. I suppose I could take him next weekend." She wore a cologne that smelled like apple blossoms. "Why don't you come with us?" he heard himself say.

"What?" She was clearly startled.

"Come with us," he repeated, hoping she wouldn't say no.

"I think you and Sean should get . . . get to know each other without any distractions."

She'd be a distraction, all right. But he could be persuasive if he chose to be. "You said language therapy is best done in a group. You can be our group."

Kelly began to laugh. The dimple showed again. "Hoist with my own petard," she said, then hesitated.

Negotiating was Grant's forte. He jumped into the breach created by her silence. Spreading his hands in mock supplication, he asked, "How am I going to learn the right way to talk to Sean without an example to follow?"

"I gave you an example this morning."

"Not enough," he said. Then before she could refuse, he added, "Please. I need your help." As he said the words, he realized they were true.

Her eyes softened. "All right. I'll come, but—"

"But, what?"

"But you'll do most of the talking," she said. "I'll give you a model to start with. Then you'll have to take over."

"Okay." He flashed her a grin. "You can consider it parent education."

"All right."

"Good," he said, rising now. "Give me your address, and I'll pick you up at two o'clock a week from Saturday. And, while we're at it, let's dispense with the formalities and start on a first-name basis. All right, Kelly?"

"Okay." Her cheeks showed a hint of a most becoming blush, and he felt an almost adolescent pleasure in the thought that he had caused it.

She scribbled the information he'd asked for on a slip of paper. When she handed it to him, their fingers brushed. A brief touch, but it whetted his appetite for more.

He put the paper in his jacket pocket and extended his hand. She put her hand in his, and his fingers closed around it. Small, smooth, firm. He knew he should let her go now, but he wanted to hold on a minute longer, wanted to savor what he felt when he touched her—a mixture of softness and strength.

The flush in her cheeks deepened, and he felt an answering warmth in his own body. A gentle warmth, the kind that signaled the beginning of spring and rebirth.

Slowly, he opened his fingers, and her hand fell

away. "Good-bye, Kelly," he said softly, turned, and left the room.

Outside, crossing the parking lot, he found himself whistling, something he rarely did nowadays. Perhaps the clear April morning prompted his lighthearted mood. *Why kid yourself?* he thought. It wasn't the weather that made him feel so cheerful but the woman he'd spent the last half hour with. A woman who could make juice and goldfish crackers seem like a rare treat. A woman with sea-green eyes and hair the color of sunrise.

How long until he'd see her again? A week from Saturday. When he got into his car, he wrote the date on his calendar.

On Thursday afternoon the entire Cedar Grove staff, from preschool on, filed into the weekly faculty meeting. Marla tapped Kelly's arm. "If you don't have any plans for the evening, how about an early dinner when we finish here?"

"Make that Mexican food, and you've got a deal."

They met at Ninfa's, a popular dining spot, where they were surrounded by the typical ambience of a Mexican restaurant—white walls, dark wooden beams, wooden chairs painted in bright colors, and the spicy smell of Mexican cuisine. They ordered margaritas and settled back to enjoy tostadas with a tangy guacamole dip.

"Ted's found some property he thinks you should see," Marla said between bites. Her fiancé headed the real estate department of one of Houston's larger banks.

"Property?"

"For your school."

"Oh, Marla. Ted's sweet to suggest it, but the school's a year off, maybe two. I don't think—"

"Wait, listen to this. The house is tied up in probate. It won't be on the market for some time."

Time! The magic word. Kelly leaned forward. "Tell me more."

"Better yet, we'll show you. why don't Ted and I pick you up Sunday morning and you can take a look at the house, say around nine-thirty?"

"Let's go at ten-thirty, and I'll spring for brunch afterward. Tell Ted thanks for thinking of me."

As Kelly continued to munch on tostadas, questions flew around in her head. Was the house in good repair? Was it occupied? Where was it located? And, most important, how much would it cost? She was so involved with her thoughts that she missed Marla's next words. Only the sound of exaggerated throat clearing got her attention. "Sorry. What did you say?"

"I said, Cathy Turner told me she saw you standing outside your room yesterday with a very attractive man."

Kelly groaned. The last thing she needed was to have Cathy spreading rumors about her. "Oh, no. That was Grant Stuart. I hope you told her he's the parent of a child I'm working with."

"I did," Marla said, "but she said the look you were giving him was definitely not the parent-teacher variety."

Kelly felt her face flame. Was she that transparent that anyone walking down the hall could see how she'd looked at Grant Stuart—as if he were a rock star and she an awed teenybopper?

"Are you attracted to him?" Marla inquired.

If someone else had asked her, Kelly would have been offended, but Marla was a dear friend and her confidante. Still, she wasn't ready to admit to any feelings for Grant Stuart, so she tried to pass the comment off lightly. "Now you sound like Cathy. 'Considering a little extracurricular activity, hmm?' " She sighed. "What can I do to keep Cathy quiet . . . aside from tying her up and gagging her?"

"Oh, I think I nipped her story in the bud," Marla

answered. "But tell me, *would* you go out with Grant if he asked?"

"No," Kelly said, on solid ground now. She was certain that no matter how attractive she found the man, she wouldn't consider getting involved. "Anyway," she went on, "your question's hypothetical. He hasn't asked me. At least not for a date. We're only going . . . that is, he only suggested . . ."

Marla grinned at Kelly's discomfort. "Yes?" she prodded.

"He asked me to go to the zoo."

"The zoo!" Marla burst out laughing. "For a little monkey business?"

"Come on, cut it out," Kelly pleaded. "He's taking Sean to the zoo and he asked me to go along, that's all."

"I assume you said yes."

"What could I say?" Kelly asked. "The man needs to learn to talk to his son. Who else is going to teach him?"

"Good point. Grant needs to learn to communicate. Why, he's the most closed-mouth, introverted—"

"Hey, go easy on the poor guy," Kelly interrupted.

"Oh, now you're feeling sorry for him again," Marla said. "Well, spare your sympathy. What Grant Stuart needs is a course in basic human emotions. He's a lousy parent."

"Maybe he's doing the best he can," Kelly objected. "He's had a tragic loss, and he's raising this child alone. Lots of men don't feel comfortable with small children. He needs to learn how to play with Sean, how to talk to him."

Marla frowned at her. "Defending him, huh? You *are* getting interested in him, aren't you?"

The feel of Grant's fingers around hers flashed through Kelly's mind. "Of course not."

"Ever hear the one about the lady protesting too much?"

"I'm serious," Kelly said. "You know me. I'd never get mixed up with someone at work. Never again."

Marla nodded. "The long arm of Nicholas the neurologist reaches out again."

"He almost ruined my career," Kelly sighed.

"He was a rat, but you're over him," Marla pointed out as their dinners arrived and they started on the juicy *tacos al carbon*. She paused between bites to give Kelly a questioning look. "You are over Nick, aren't you?"

"Of course I am. That was almost five years ago."

"Right. Let's talk about the present. Even if you're not interested, Grant must be or he wouldn't have asked you to go with him and Sean."

For just a moment when he'd taken her hand, she'd thought she'd seen a spark of interest in his eyes, but that had undoubtedly been a trick of her overactive imagination. She shook her head. "I suggested to Grant that he take Sean to the zoo, and since he doesn't know how to interact with Sean, I'm going along to hold his hand."

When Marla gave a whoop of laughter, Kelly protested, "Figuratively. I'm acting as a role model. Grant . . . Mr. Stuart, that is . . . has shown about as much interest in me as a vegetarian at a meat counter."

Marla raised a brow. "Oh? Cathy said he didn't look so disinterested the other morning." When Kelly snorted, she went on, "Regardless of my personal feelings about him, which I admit are based on his parenting skills, Grant *is* attractive. And sexy." She hummed a few bars of "This Could Be the Start of Something Big" and grinned at Kelly.

"Ridiculous," Kelly said, pointing her fork at Marla. "Besides, what could happen in front of the monkey cage in broad daylight with a three-year-old along?"

Marla rolled her eyes and leered at Kelly. "Wanna hear my fantasy? Okay, okay," she said when Kelly shook her head. "We'll talk about something else." She set her face in serious lines. "What's your opinion of heterogeneous grouping of age levels in the preschool population?"

Grant pushed the elevator button for the twentieth floor. He was tired and tense. Boston, as usual, had been busy, thanks to strained negotiations with the anchor tenant in the new shopping center. He rubbed the back of his neck in a futile effort to dispel the tightness.

He was exhausted from being up too late last night. He'd spent the evening with a woman he dated occasionally when he was here, but now he wondered why he'd bothered. Diana was blond and svelte, sophisticated and witty . . . and much more interested in what was in his wallet than what was in his soul. *Damn*, he thought, as the elevator doors slid open to reveal a richly carpeted hallway. Why did he always wind up with Claudia clones? Was he looking for an encore? *When hell freezes over,* he thought. No second time around for him. The first had been more than anyone should have to suffer.

Maybe he should go back down to the bar and have a stiff drink, he thought as he reached in his pocket for his room key. Then his hand closed over a scrap of paper and he changed his mind. Quickly he slid the key into the lock, opened the door, and shrugged off his jacket, loosened his tie, and kicked off his shoes. Stretching out on the bed, he stared at the paper. Why not call her? She'd intruded on his thoughts often enough this last week. He reached for the phone.

Kelly was curled up on her couch eating popcorn and watching an old Hitchcock movie when the phone rang. She uttered an unladylike epithet. "Just at the best part!" She pushed Walter out of the way and reached for the receiver. "Hello."

"Kelly."

That mellow voice again. "Mr. Stu . . . Grant. I thought you were in Boston."

He was inordinately pleased that she'd recognized his voice. "I am."

Was he calling to cancel their zoo plans? No way she'd let him get away with that. She'd tell him what she thought—too busy to take time for his son! "Why are you calling?" she asked.

Grant figured she thought he was canceling their trip to the zoo. And, from the sound of her voice, she was going to give him hell. He pictured her eyes flashing emerald sparks and grinned. "I'm . . . I'm calling because—" Why *was* he calling? *Because I'm lonely.* "I . . . ah . . . wanted to know how Sean's therapy is going."

"Oh." She attributed the feeling of relief that flowed through her to the knowledge that Sean would have some time with his father. "He's doing just fine," she said. "He's learned three more words—*ball, car,* and *fish.* I've gotten out my zoo toys, and now we're working on *bear* and *monkey.*"

Grant chuckled and settled back, aware that his tension was fading. "You sound delighted. You must love your work."

"I do. Don't you? Love yours, I mean."

"I wouldn't term it 'love,' but yes, I enjoy it."

Kelly bent to put the bowl of popcorn on the floor, tossed a few kernels to a grateful Walter, then plumped up a throw pillow and lay back on the couch. "What do you do exactly?"

Grant unbuttoned his shirt and pulled it from his trousers. With the toe of his left foot, he inched the sock off his right. "I do deals—land deals, money deals, landlord-tenant deals. Today I signed long-term leases with a bookstore and a jewelry store for a mall I'm developing."

Kelly liked listening to him talk. She tried to picture

him. Was he sitting at a desk, wearing his usual tailored suit? ''Your work sounds interesting.''

''And stressful,'' he replied, thinking of the entire afternoon spent discussing two minor points in the lease with the department store that would be his major tenant.

''What do you do to relax?''

''Go out to my ranch, ride, work with the horses.''

That explained the calluses on his hands. ''How wonderful to have a ranch. Do you go often?''

''Not often enough.''

''Well, if you get too stressed out and want to change careers, you could always get work as a radio disc jockey. You have the voice for it. Distinctive.'' *Seductive.*

He felt foolishly pleased, but he told himself she'd noticed because she specialized in voices. ''Really?''

''Yes, it's that Southern drawl.''

''Perhaps I should schedule some sessions with you to get rid of it.''

''Oh, no. It's very attractive.'' She heard his triumphant male chuckle and added, ''As I'm sure you know.''

He laughed again. How long since he'd enjoyed a silly, pointless conversation so much? ''I never tire of compliments.''

Kelly paused with her hand midway between the popcorn bowl and her mouth. What was she doing, getting personal with a client? What was happening to her iron-clad policy? She cleared her throat. ''Well, I . . . I have to go. I'll see you Saturday.''

''I'm looking forward to it. Two o'clock.''

His voice had deepened several notes. Kelly felt a wave of heat that seemed to radiate from the receiver all through her body. ''Two o'clock,'' she repeated.

Grant hung up the phone and lay back, hands behind his head. He smiled lazily. Talking to Kelly had done more for him than a drink, and although he'd never taken one, he was certain she'd been better for him than a tranquilizer. For the first time since he'd arrived in Boston, he was completely relaxed.

Kelly stared at the receiver in her hand. If a simple telephone call could set her pulse pounding this way, she wondered what *could* happen in front of the monkey cage in broad daylight with a three-year-old along.

FOUR

Kelly sat at her desk, trying to read a report and keep one ear tuned to the door. Sean's grandparents were in Houston, and they'd requested an appointment. They should be here any minute.

She hoped they were the warm, caring people Sean needed—the kind of grandparents who'd cuddle him, read him stories, take him fishing. Not someone distant like—

She heard the knock and called, "Come in."

Pat Ferris opened the door. Behind her stood a middle-aged couple—an elegant woman whose shoulder-length blond hair showed streaks of silver and a tall, distinguished gentleman. Pat introduced Nancy and Joe Hamilton, then left.

The Hamiltons didn't look like the cuddly kind of grandparents, but at least they'd been interested enough to visit Sean's school.

Nancy Hamilton sat down gracefully, smoothed her designer silk dress, and began the conversation. "We've just come into town. Joe has been based in Japan the last few years, so we haven't had a chance to spend any time with Sean. When we arrived, Grant was out of town, but the housekeeper told us about

Sean's . . . ah, problem . . . and mentioned that you were tutoring him."

Kelly cringed inwardly. She hated being referred to as a tutor. "I've seen him for therapy for the past six weeks."

"We're grateful something's being done about the problem," Mr. Hamilton said. "Of course, we wanted to meet you."

Look me over, Kelly thought. Well, that was all right. Families had every right to evaluate their child's clinician. But in this case, the choice was Grant's.

"You've seen Sean for only six weeks," Mr. Hamilton said. "Did someone else work with him before that?"

"No."

"But surely it was evident the child wasn't developing as he should," protested Mrs. Hamilton.

"I don't think so," Kelly said. "His teacher, Ms. Howard, noticed he wasn't talking and—"

"His teacher?" Mrs. Hamilton interrupted. "You mean his father didn't realize Sean had a problem?"

Kelly could have bitten her tongue. While she privately agreed that Grant should have noticed, she knew she shouldn't have planted this idea in the Hamiltons' minds.

Now she felt compelled to defend Grant. "With first children, parents often aren't aware of developmental milestones, so many overlook a delay in language."

Mrs. Hamilton raised a sculpted brow. She was an attractive woman, Kelly thought, with her fair hair and sapphire blue eyes. She'd heard Sean's mother was pretty. Looking at his grandmother and projecting back twenty years or so, she concluded that Claudia Stuart must have been stunning.

Now the grandmother tapped a manicured fingernail on the side of the desk. "You don't think Sean is . . . retarded, do you?"

"Of course not. Just language delayed."

"I see." Mrs. Hamilton paused for a moment, then said, "Ms. Connery, just how *do* children learn to speak?"

"In layman's terms, please," Joe Hamilton added.

"To give you a simple explanation of a very complex process, they learn by hearing and interacting with other people."

"And if they don't . . . hear other people talk or have someone to interact with?" Mrs. Hamilton inquired.

Kelly sensed what the woman meant. "Mrs. Hamilton, rarely does a child have a total lack of interaction with adults."

"Of course," Mrs. Hamilton said. "Even Sean has the housekeeper. She said you've given her suggestions to help him."

"Yes, she comes in once a week."

"And Sean's father? Does he come in?" Mr. Hamilton asked.

"He has been in, yes."

"Weekly?"

"He's out of town a great deal. I've seen him three times." If she counted the conference and their conversation in the rain, her statement was true. "Sean's already had his session today," she said, anxious to change the subject, "or I'd invite you to sit in. Perhaps we can schedule a time soon."

"We'd like that," Mr. Hamilton said. "We'll do everything we can to help him. You will give us suggestions, won't you?"

"Dozens," Kelly promised, pleased that the Hamiltons seemed sincerely interested in doing their part to help Sean.

"Let's plan on tomorrow," Mrs. Hamilton suggested.

Kelly mentally ran down her schedule. "I'm afraid I won't have much extra time. I'm retesting a child, and I have a parent conference, so I may have to squeeze Sean in where someone's absent.''

Both the Hamiltons looked disappointed. ''Our time in Houston is limited,'' Mrs. Hamilton said. ''We want every minute to count. We can meet after school.''

''Of course we'll compensate you for your time,'' Mr. Hamilton added.

Compensation didn't concern her. She'd made a dentist appointment for tomorrow afternoon, but she could see that the Hamiltons, pleasant though they were, were demanding. They wouldn't be satisfied with a no. Besides, she could hardly fault them for wanting to help Sean. ''All right,'' she said. ''We can get together at three and take Sean to the park.'' She'd have that tooth filled another time.

''We're leaving early next week,'' Mrs. Hamilton continued. ''But we'll be returning to Houston for a couple of months this summer, and then we want to spend as much time with Sean as we can. I feel so badly that we've missed these early years. I want to make up for lost time.'' She paused and her eyes misted. ''He looks so much like our daughter when she was small.''

Kelly's heart softened. This woman had lost so much. ''I'll demonstrate some things to do with Sean tomorrow, and you can call me when you come back. I won't be working with Sean in the summer, but I can give you suggestions for ways to help him.''

''You don't continue in the summer?'' Mr. Hamilton said. ''Won't Sean lose ground?''

''The school is closed, and I substitute at Children's Hospital during summer vacation,'' Kelly explained. ''But I'll give Mr. Stuart a list of private clinics in the area that can provide summer therapy. I'm sure whoever works with Sean would welcome your interest.''

''Wonderful,'' Mrs. Hamilton said. ''Sean is very precious to us, as I'm sure you understand.''

The Hamiltons rose and said good-bye, promising to be back at three sharp the next day.

After they left, Kelly sat staring at the door, her report forgotten. She was glad the Hamiltons would become part of Sean's life. They would do more than stimulate his language, she felt sure. They would offer warmth and love, something he sorely needed. She wouldn't accuse Grant of not loving Sean—he must care for his son in his own way—but he had such difficulty expressing his feelings.

Again her thoughts returned to the old photograph of Grant. Since it had been taken, he'd built a wall between himself and the world. Why? To protect himself from further pain? To insulate himself from feelings of any kind? If only she could scale that wall and make him see how much Sean needed him. Maybe on Saturday she could make a start.

At quarter to two on Saturday Kelly sat in front of her mirror, combing her hair for the third time. Scowling at her reflection, she cursed her naturally curly hair, which seemed to have a mind of its own. She'd have to settle for the windblown look. Not that her hair should matter. But, of course, she always preferred to look her best when meeting with a client.

Especially this client? inquired a little voice within her.

Any client, Kelly insisted. In the mirror she saw her cheeks flush, a sure sign she was lying to herself. Disgusted, she tossed down her brush and stalked away from the dresser, only to return a moment later to check her makeup.

"Cut it out!" she ordered herself and went into the living room, where she picked up several typed sheets of paper with information for Grant. She was checking them over when the doorbell rang.

When she saw Grant, her mouth almost dropped open. Attired in a plaid shirt, open at the throat, and jeans that outlined every male inch of him, he looked so much like the Grant Stuart of the old snapshot, she could hardly believe her eyes.

"You look surprised. Weren't you expecting me?" he asked.

"Yes, but you . . . ah, look different," she blurted. "I mean . . . the jeans—" Embarrassed, she broke off.

Grant frowned. "They seemed appropriate for the zoo. Did you expect black tie?"

Her embarrassment forgotten, Kelly chuckled, "No, of course not, but I've always seen you in a suit."

"It's not permanently attached. I do take it off occasionally," he muttered, looking annoyed. "Are you ready?"

She nodded, then realized he was alone. "Where's Sean?"

"Olivia put him down for a nap. I had an errand to run, so I stopped here on the way back. We'll pick him up now."

In the car, Kelly settled back against the leather seat and studied Grant. Though he was dressed as he'd been in the photograph, his demeanor was entirely different. No longer did he wear that easy air of laughter and *joie de vivre*. Now he was somber, his mouth set in serious lines. Even his hands on the steering wheel looked tense.

Kelly's heart went out to him. Was he thinking of his wife, wishing she were here to join him on this outing? Was he having problems in his business? She wanted to lighten his mood.

Of course, her concern was for Sean, she told herself. Grant's attitude couldn't be good for the child. No wonder Sean's language was limited. With such a taciturn father, he wouldn't have much of a model to emulate.

But her feelings, she realized, went beyond concern for the child. She longed to reach out to Grant, wished she could smooth away the lines of care etched so deeply in his brow.

What was she thinking? These emotions were out of place. She needed to talk—about language, about the weather, about anything that would keep her mind off her desire to touch the man beside her. *Right, Kelly. Talk. Cheer him up with words, not actions.* "Did you enjoy Boston?" she inquired, seizing upon the first topic that came to mind. "I envy your going so often. It's such an interesting city."

"Maybe for tourists. I don't see much beyond the construction site." When he glanced at her, vulnerability showed on his face.

He's lonely, Kelly thought. *Busy, but lonely, and he doesn't realize it shows.* "How is the mall coming along?" she inquired.

"As well as can be expected."

That told her nothing. Well, she was a communication specialist, wasn't she? She'd manage somehow to keep the conversation going. "Is it almost finished?"

He shook his head. "We're three months behind schedule."

She heard the frustration in his voice, saw it in the set of his shoulders. Clearly, talking about his work didn't improve his mood. She changed the subject. "I met Sean's grandparents the other day. In fact, I've seen them twice. They took Sean to the park, and I went along as coach—like I'm doing today."

"Mmm. Olivia told me they were in town. They'll be moving back to San Francisco from Japan soon."

Two sentences. She'd made progress. "What does Mr. Hamilton do in Japan?"

"He's a partner in a company that imports Asian art."

"That must be interesting. How long have they been there?"

"Four years this go-around," Grant replied.

They hadn't seen much of Sean then. Or perhaps

they made frequent trips back and forth. "Do they come back often?"

"Joe makes occasional business trips, but Nancy's only been back twice—once two years ago, and once . . . just after Sean was born."

When Claudia died, Kelly thought. She didn't want to pursue that line of discussion, and judging by the set of his jaw, neither did Grant. She steered the conversation to safer ground. "The Hamiltons are fortunate to be able to know another country."

Grant laughed mirthlessly. "Joe may have learned about the country—he needs to learn the culture—but I doubt Nancy has. She's the sort of person who'd look around her and say, 'Would you believe it—these people are speaking Japanese?' "

Grant's comment surprised Kelly. Nancy hadn't impressed her that way at all, but then, their conversations had focused on Sean. She wondered about Grant's relationship with his in-laws. *None of your business, Kelly*.

Time for another change of subject. "Is Sean looking forward to the zoo?"

Grant nodded.

"And you?"

He chuckled. "Are you kidding?"

Kelly laughed and shook her head. "The zoo's a great place."

He looked surprised. "Are you speaking from experience?"

Relieved to have found a neutral topic that sparked Grant's interest, Kelly replied, "I went a couple of months ago with a fourth-grade boy I work with. He had to do a report on changes in Houston and he decided to write about the new sea lion pool."

"You were working with him on *writing*?"

People always assumed speech pathologists did nothing but work with stutterers. "Of course," she explained. "Writing is language, too."

"I suppose you're right."

"Yes, and so's reading."

"And I thought you spent all your time blowing bubbles." He smiled for the first time.

Kelly felt her heart flutter. She was certain Grant rarely smiled, but when he did, his face was transformed. He had the kind of grin that made a woman's heart beat in double time.

They stopped for a traffic light. Grant turned and their eyes met, his alight with humor. "Bubbles," Kelly repeated, shaking her head, and together they began to laugh.

Kelly leaned back against the seat. "You know," she murmured, "I have a feeling that beneath that grim exterior is a nice man trying to get out." As soon as she spoke, she realized with dismay that she'd discarded her professional mien. Her tone had been . . . flirtatious.

Grant glanced at her and raised a brow. His eyes were no longer laughter-filled, but dark and appraising. Suddenly, she sensed him looking at her, not as his son's clinician, but as a woman. Something simmered between them, something electric and exciting that skimmed along her nerve endings. Kelly swallowed. Why had she come out with that teasing remark? She'd altered their relationship, and if she wanted to steer it back to a professional one, she'd better do it now.

She cleared her throat. "I . . . ah, brought you information on language stimulation, some techniques you can use at home, and a list of private clinics that can provide services this summer."

Grant glanced at her again. "You know," he said, his voice a silken murmur, "I have a feeling that beneath that professional exterior is a woman trying to get out."

A blush flooded her cheeks. She didn't know how to deal with this side of Grant Stuart.

Then a driver behind them honked, and Grant looked away. Embarrassed and uncertain what to say, Kelly remained silent until they turned down a tree-lined street in the prestigious River Oaks area. Grant pulled into the wide, curving driveway of a two-story house with a mansard roof and white columns on its broad porch. The spacious lawn was landscaped with wax leaf ligustrum, oleander, and fuchsia azaleas. Wisteria bushes trailed purple blooms against the white brick.

Thankful for the chance to restore their equilibrium, Kelly said, "Your house is lovely."

"Thanks."

He got out of the car and strode around to her side. She was about to get out when he extended his hand to help her from the car. For an instant, Kelly sat frozen. She didn't want him to touch her. No, that wasn't true; she wanted his touch . . . too much. She glanced up and saw a lazy smile, a teasing warmth in his eyes. "Coming?" he asked.

He didn't leave her any choice. She put her hand in his and felt the roughness, the strength. She wondered if he could feel the pulse pounding at her wrist. When she stood beside him, he released her and put his hand at her back to guide her across the porch. Immediately her focus shifted. Though the touch at her waist was light, she felt it through her entire body.

In the marble-tiled entry hall, he dropped his hand. "I'll get Sean," he said. "Make yourself at home."

Kelly was glad she didn't have to answer. Being this close to Grant interfered with the function of her vocal cords. She watched him head up the stairs, unable to tear her eyes from the view of chestnut brown hair curling above a western collar, broad shoulders, tight masculine buttocks, and—

Disgusted, she composed Connery's Second Commandment: Thou shalt not covet thy student's father . . . and promised herself she'd abide by it. Satisfied with her resolution, she directed her thoughts to the house instead of its owner.

She walked into the living room, where sheer elegance met her eyes. French antique furniture, porcelain, and crystal objets d'art, Asian pieces that must have come from the Hamiltons. Beautiful, untouchable, impersonal. No clutter, no mementos of the people living here. The room was so perfect, Kelly wondered if it was ever used.

The living room opened into a small study. Kelly strolled in and paused. On the wall hung a painting of a woman. Kelly walked toward it, mesmerized. *Claudia Stuart*, she thought, gazing at the portrait. Claudia's eyes were a deep violet-blue, her skin a flawless ivory, her hair a molten gold that fell around her face in glorious waves. Her lips were parted in a provocative half-smile that seemed to whisper . . . promises. Although her iridescent silk gown was simple, even modest, the tilt of Claudia's head, the curve of her arm, the look in her eyes belied the propriety of the dress and hinted of dark pleasures, secret delights.

Here was a woman who could capture a man at first glance and hold him in thrall forever after. Kelly let out a tremulous breath. No wonder Grant's face bore the ravages of pain. He'd never gotten over Claudia's death. Perhaps he never would.

Sounds from the entry hall drew her attention, and she stepped back, loath to be caught intruding on Grant's private life. She hurried through the living room and out to the hallway. Grant stood in the doorway, waiting for Sean, who scampered down the stairs. At the sight of Kelly, the little boy broke into a thousand-watt smile. "Ke-ee!" he cried.

"Hi, Sean." She opened her arms and he ran into them. She lifted him up for a hug, then set him down. "Ready for the zoo?"

Sean shook his head and tugged at her arm. "Up," he demanded, turning back toward the stairs.

"He wants to show you his room," Olivia, who had followed him downstairs, explained.

"I'll just be a minute," she told Grant and followed Sean upstairs. His room contained everything a small boy's should have—bunk beds crowded with stuffed animals, shelves of picture books, a toy chest opened to reveal race cars and Lego blocks, a chalkboard, a rocking horse. Kelly was glad. The downstairs looked as if no child could exist there; in fact, she wondered if an adult would be comfortable in such surroundings. She hadn't seen a spot where you could take off your shoes, curl up, and relax. Perhaps that explained Grant's habitual air of coiled tension.

She followed Sean about the room as he pointed to his bed and his toys, proudly proclaiming each item "mine."

On the shelf stood a set of wooden zoo animals. "I bought him those," Olivia told her, "to get him ready for today."

The woman did everything possible to fill Sean's life with love and language. Kelly gave her a grateful smile, then took Sean's hand. "Come on. Time to see those monkeys."

Downstairs, she said, "Tell Daddy we're ready to go."

"Go!" Sean responded.

"Tell Sean we're going in the car," she instructed Grant.

He obediently echoed, "We're going in the car, Sean."

Patiently, Kelly demonstrated the short, simple sentences Sean would understand, but Grant persisted in addressing Sean as if he were an adult. He was bound to catch on, Kelly told herself. Surely he could learn.

Or maybe he couldn't, she decided, when they arrived at the Hermann Park Zoo fifteen minutes later. She decided to attack the problem directly. "Loosen up, Dad," she whispered. "We're supposed to be having fun. And you're supposed to be talking. Short sentences, remember? He's only three."

"I'm trying." He sounded frustrated.

Kelly sighed but refused to let him curb her normal

enthusiasm. Out of the car, she spun in a circle. "It's a beautiful day."

Grant stared at her. Arms outspread, face raised to the sky, she made an enchanting picture. She seemed to delight in life and living, and her exuberance was catching. For the first time that day, he looked around and noticed the gentle blue of the sky, the green of new leaves on majestic oaks, the sweet April breeze that ruffled Kelly's hair. He smiled, a genuine, from-the-heart response to the day and the woman beside him.

She took Sean's right hand, and following her lead, he took the left. The child's fingers curled about his. Grant felt a flash of longing. If only he could enjoy this day the way any other father would.

He brushed the thought aside and concentrated on what Kelly said to Sean. As she'd done in the car, she talked to him constantly, filling her voice with excitement.

She had a nice voice, he thought—clear and sweet. He gazed at her, enjoying the outline of gently rounded breasts beneath her T-shirt. Form-fitting jeans showed off her trim waist and long, slim legs. Altogether an appealing combination. So unlike Claudia with her lush curves, her sultry, come-hither air. Claudia, whose every move was calculated. Kelly Connery, on the other hand, seemed natural and unaffected.

"—first?"

"What?" He'd completely missed what she'd said.

"I said, shall we start with the reptile house and the small mammals, or head straight for the monkeys?"

He shrugged. "You're the boss."

"Oh, no." She grinned. "This is *your* outing, remember?"

She was right, but he couldn't help feeling uncomfortable. "I'd . . . uh, welcome your opinion."

Kelly laughed. "Okay. Monkeys first. Then you're on your own." She turned to Sean. "Monkeys!"

"Muk—ee," Sean echoed.

The monkey cages were surrounded by crowds of children, but they managed to edge to the front, where Sean could see. He was delighted. "Muk—ee," he squealed, as the animals swung from branch to branch, groomed one another, and chattered.

Grant looked at Kelly, but she raised her brows, stepped back, and indicated that he should take over. He felt like a monkey himself. What did he know about talking to children? Awkwardly, he crouched down until he was eye level with Sean and pointed to the cage. "See that one," he said.

"Dat!" Sean agreed.

"And that one." Damn, he hadn't felt this ill at ease since he'd had to sing a solo in the seventh-grade Christmas pageant and worried if his voice would crack. He looked up at Kelly.

She leaned back against the rail and met his gaze with a mischievous smile. "You're doing fine."

He stared at her, captured by the sparkle in her eyes, and felt himself drowning in their clear green depths. Something caught in his chest, something barely familiar. Emotion. To a man who had shut off all emotion for three long years, the feeling was at once alien and heady. He continued to look at Kelly, unable to tear his eyes away.

Slowly, he rose. He wanted to touch her, brush his fingers across her cheek, run them through the mass of curls that framed her face, breathe in her alluring scent. Heedless of their surroundings, he moved toward her—

From somewhere far away, he felt a tug at his arm. As if waking from a dream, he glanced down. Sean pulled at him.

"Beh," the child said.

"Uh . . . more monkeys," Grant said, wrenching himself back to the present.

"Beh!" The child's voice showed irritation.

"Beh?" Grant muttered, unable to decipher the meaning.

"He wants to see the bears," Kelly said.

"Oh." Grateful for an interpreter, Grant followed Kelly to the bear pits. He'd sort through his feelings later. Now he'd concentrate on the zoo and talking to Sean.

He tried his best. He made an effort to emulate Kelly's conversational style, alien though it felt. Gamely, he endured all the sights, sounds, and smells of the zoo—shouting children, squalling babies, popcorn, cotton candy, balloons. After the bears they visited alligators, tigers, elephants, even the hippo, whose odoriferous enclosure he could have skipped.

Kelly, of course, seemed at home here. She watched the animals with as much enthusiasm as Sean, helped him toss food to the bears, exclaimed over the alligators, and joined Sean in stroking the llama in the petting area. She seemed to enjoy every moment of the zoo. Or was she putting on a show for him, as Claudia would have done? He rejected that thought. Claudia wouldn't have come here at all. Zoos weren't her turf, and even for her own child, he doubted she'd have made the effort.

They bought cotton candy and strolled along munching. "Makes me feel like a kid," Kelly said when she finished hers.

"You look like a kid," Grant said, smiling down at her. "You even have candy on your cheek." He stopped her. "Right there," he murmured and wiped it away with his fingertip. Her skin was satin smooth. The feel could become addicting.

He heard Kelly's breath catch, saw her eyes widen. She was as affected by the touch as he. Something else to mull over.

When Sean had finished his treat, they stopped at a water fountain spurting from the mouth of a huge plaster lion. To get a drink, Sean had to put his head in the lion's mouth, an experience that reduced him to a fit of giggles. He took another drink, backed off to look at the lion, then started forward again. "More," he said.

"Let's go, Sean," Grant suggested. Much more time in the lion's mouth would result in more visits to the bathroom than he cared to make. At least, Sean had added the word *potty* to his vocabulary, saving Grant from having to guess. He took Sean's hand. "Come on," he urged.

The child dug in his heels. "More," he said. "More water."

"Oh, Grant." Kelly's eyes gleamed with delight. "He put two words together! This is a milestone!"

Grant realized he was supposed to be impressed. He made what he hoped were approving noises as Kelly drew Sean away, saying, "Yes, more water. Let's get another drink."

Kelly watched Sean turn the faucet off and on, enjoying the way the water splattered over the lion's tongue. He wasn't thirsty, she saw, just fascinated with the water fountain.

She turned and glanced at Grant, who waited stiffly behind them. He really was out of his element. She supposed she ought to take pity on him, but just now she was too angry. She'd spent the day—her day off—pulling teeth to get him to interact with Sean. Then, when the child made a real breakthrough, Grant acted as if he hardly cared. Biting back an angry lecture, she turned to Sean and took his hand. "You're finished."

"More," the child insisted.

"No more," Kelly said. "Let's go see the birds." Immediately intrigued, Sean complied.

"I thought we'd be at the water fountain all day. How'd you get him away?" Grant asked.

Kelly shrugged. "Easy. I got him interested in something else. Works every time." She started to suggest he keep that in mind for future outings, then snapped her lips shut. He probably wouldn't plan any.

When they reached the birdhouse, Sean became absorbed. Kelly watched him but thought about Grant. A perplexing man. Handsome, sophisticated, but uncommunicative and uncomfortable with his child, perhaps with all personal relationships. *And when did you become a psychiatrist, Ms. Connery? Grant Stuart's not your problem except in relation to Sean. Keep that in mind.* She bent down. "Enough birds, Sean?"

The child looked up and yawned. "Enough zoo," Kelly decided. She glanced at Grant, but he was lost in thought. She fought back an urge to elbow him in the ribs. "Why don't you tell him it's time to go?" she said.

"Time to go," Grant repeated.

Kelly gave a sigh of frustration. The man was a lost cause. No originality. No better than the parrots in the cage before them. She took Sean's hand and forestalled the pout she could see emerging. "You can come back. Now we're going home."

Sean yawned again. As they headed for the exit, his footsteps dragged. Kelly was surprised when Grant looked down at the tired youngster, then lifted him into his arms. Sean put his thumb in his mouth and snuggled against his father. Kelly smiled at the sleepy child, his face smudged with dirt and cotton candy, his mouth working rhythmically at his thumb, his head resting against Grant's broad shoulder.

For the first time since she'd seen them together, Grant seemed relaxed with Sean. She even saw a tentative smile cross his face as he settled his son against his shoulder. *Good,* Kelly thought. They'd made a step after all . . . a very small one, but a step nevertheless, and in the right direction.

As they walked, Grant turned to Kelly. "You were excited back there when he said . . . what? . . . 'more water.' "

She nodded.

"Why?"

Kelly frowned at him as though the reason were so obvious he shouldn't have to ask. "I told you, putting two words together is an important milestone."

"You really seem to care," he said.

"Of course I care," she answered.

"But he's only your *student*."

Kelly smiled gently. "He doesn't have to be my own child for me to care about him."

Grant regarded her thoughtfully, then turned away, mulling over her words. The idea was foreign to him, but it, too, was something to ponder.

He glanced at Sean and felt the weight of the child in his arms, the softness of Sean's hair against his cheek, the tickle of breath against his neck. He carried the boy to the car, set him down in his car seat, and watched as Sean sighed sleepily and shut his eyes. For a moment Grant's heart opened, and an unfamiliar tenderness invaded him as he looked at the peacefully sleeping child.

Shaken, he got into his seat. He wasn't used to these feelings, wasn't sure he was ready for them. Not so many, so fast. Feeling battered and vulnerable, he clamped the lid down on his emotions.

Kelly smiled as she got into the car. "He's exhausted," she whispered.

"Yeah," Grant said gruffly.

"He had a wonderful time," Kelly went on. "He learned so much, and being with you was good for him. He needs family."

"Family," Grant repeated as if the word were new to him. Then he shook his head, banishing the tenderness that threatened to overwhelm him. "What you see is what he gets."

Kelly heard the anguish behind the brusque words. As Grant backed out of the parking lot, she pondered his statement and wondered at the emotions it masked.

They were both silent on the way home. Grant seemed lost in thought, and behind them, Sean slept. When they arrived at her condo she reached for the door handle.

"I appreciate your spending the afternoon with me . . . with us," Grant told her as she got out of the car.

"I was glad to. Tell Sean bye for me. And keep talking to him."

He nodded and drove away.

Kelly watched the car move down the street, hoping that Grant would heed her words. She wanted him to spend time with Sean, talk to him, play with him. Because she'd meant what she'd said. Sean did need family, and if his only family was a father, it would be nice if the man would learn how to love.

FIVE

The next morning Kelly awoke with a weight on her chest and a rumble in her ears. Sometime during the night twelve pounds of cat had decided to camp out on her. She opened her eyes and stared into a pair of green ones. "Morning, Walter," she mumbled.

The rumble got louder.

"Get off me, you beast." Kelly sat up, dislodged the cat, and swung her legs off the bed. Walter rubbed against her, then looked up and meowed.

"Okay. Breakfast time." She padded out to the kitchen and Walter followed, meowing plaintively.

"Anyone listening would think you hadn't been fed for months," Kelly grumbled. "I'd be charged with cat abuse." She filled his dish. Walter dived in.

"You're welcome," Kelly muttered. She fixed coffee, curled up on the couch for a leisurely hour with the Sunday paper, then got ready for her outing with Ted and Marla.

When they were on their way, she turned to Ted. "Tell me about the house. Where is it? How old is it? What—"

"Whoa!" He held up a hand. "Wait until you see it. Then you can ask me anything you want. Help me out, honey," he said to Marla. "Talk to her about something else."

"Okay. How was the zoo?"

"Fine. Sean had a wonderful time."

"I'm sure he did, but how about the main attraction?"

"Hmm?"

"You know who I mean. Daddy. The hunk. How did he behave at the zoo—like a teddy bear or a wolf?"

Kelly smiled wryly. "He made a monkey of himself."

"What happened?"

Kelly sighed, remembering her frustration during the outing. "Yesterday was the exact opposite of my session with Sean's grandparents. When we went to the park with Nancy Hamilton, she plunged right in—ran in the grass, pushed Sean on the swing, even rode on the seesaw in her silk pants. And she said all the right things in the right way. But Grant doesn't have a clue about how to act with Sean, how to be close with him. I think he wants to. I saw him reaching out to Sean, then pulling back at the last minute. The man's suffering, and I don't know why."

"Maybe you'll never know," Marla said. "Kelly, you're getting too involved with this family. You have to keep your distance."

Marla was right. Kelly cared about all the children she worked with and rejoiced in their progress yet could still remain objective; but Sean had claimed a special place in her heart. And Grant, frustrating, infuriating Grant had become important to her, too. Confused by her feelings, she stared, unseeing, out the window.

A few minutes later Ted pulled up before a large brick house. "Here we are," he announced. "What do you think?"

"Fantastic!" Kelly said. She got out of the car, stood in the front yard, and looked about her. Two-storied, white with green shuttered windows, the house was surrounded by a wide expanse of lawn. "I love it."

Marla shook her head. "You haven't even looked inside. Maybe the plaster is falling off the walls, maybe the ceiling's caving in. Maybe," she added ominously, "it has termites."

"No, Ted wouldn't show me a house with termites, would you?"

"Never. Come on, let's go in." He unlocked the door. Inside, Kelly stared. On her right was a large sunny room with wide windows, on her left a smaller room with built-in bookshelves. The walls were newly painted, the hardwood floors shone. The living room would make a perfect classroom. She spun around. "Oh, Ted. It's just what I've been dreaming of." With Ted and Marla at her heels, she went through every room. "How long has it been vacant? And why?"

"The owner fixed up the house, planning to sell it. But he had a stroke and died before he could put it on the market. Now, everything's tied up in probate, but the heirs still plan to sell when the estate's settled. Should be another six months."

"They must want a fortune for it," Kelly said, looking wistfully at the glass-fronted cabinets in the breakfast room and imagining them filled with toys.

"No," Ted said. "They need cash. The asking price could change if the market goes up, but now it's low."

He named a figure, and Kelly gave a gasp of delight. The price was reasonable. "They're crazy to ask so little. The house is a treasure."

"What do you think?" Marla asked. "Can you swing it?"

Kelly took a deep breath. "If I make what I expect to this summer, I can manage a down payment with enough left over for equipment and start-up funds. Ted, what do I have to do?"

"Nothing right now. I'll let you know when the family's ready to sell."

"Oh, God, I can't believe this. Marla, can I kiss him?"

"Just a peck on the cheek."

Kelly did better. She gave Ted an exuberant hug and a noisy smack. Then she danced away. "Let's go look at the backyard.

The yard was big, shaded by oak and maple and bordered with hawthorn and azaleas, their blooms painting the lawn with spring colors. Kelly could already see swings under the oaks, a sandbox in one corner, a cement tricycle track. She visualized the yard filled with children, and a lump rose in her throat. "Marla," she said, "watch out. I think I'm in love with your fiancé."

Marla laughed. "I'll keep an eye on you. And on him."

They took a quick second tour through the house, locked up, and went out for brunch. When Ted and Marla dropped her at home afterward, Kelly was still euphoric. TLC—The Language Center—was on its way.

When Kelly arrived home Monday afternoon, the phone was ringing. She dashed across the room and picked it up. "Hello."

"Kelly, this is Harriet Barber."

"Harriet, how are you?" Kelly was delighted to hear from Harriet, the director of speech pathology at Children's Hospital. She'd enjoyed working on Harriet's staff the past few summers.

"Fine, but I have bad news."

Kelly sat down abruptly. "What?" A sinking feeling began in her stomach.

"I'm afraid we won't be able to hire you this summer. We've just gotten a new full-time person, and until her caseload builds up, she'll substitute for clinicians on vacation."

"I see," Kelly said. Her body felt numb.

"I'm sorry," Harriet went on. "I hope you realize

my decision was strictly an administrative one. We've been pleased with your work in the past. Maybe we can arrange something next year. Call me around February."

"I will. Thanks for calling." Kelly stared at the receiver in her hand. "Damn, damn, damn," she said, startling Walter with her vehemence. This couldn't have happened at a worse time. Just when she'd found the perfect house in the perfect location. Just when she needed the summer salary so badly.

Well, she wasn't going to let this setback ruin her plans. This was only the middle of April. Plenty of time to find something else. And she *would* find something. She opened the telephone directory. She could still make a few calls today about summer employment.

Two weeks later Kelly decided she wasn't going to find a summer position. "Not as a speech pathologist," she told Marla as they walked down the hall toward their classrooms. "I've called every private clinic I can think of, half a dozen hospitals, two day care centers, and eight nursing homes. Either they already have a substitute lined up or they don't need anyone at all. One place could use me three days in July. That's it. I've even called Dallas and San Antonio. Nothing."

"What're you going to do?"

"I don't have many options. I can sign up with a temporary employment agency and do office work or become a cat burglar. So I guess it's the office work. Dammit, Marla, I was really counting on that summer salary."

"Why don't you talk to your folks?" Marla suggested. "I'm sure they'd lend you the money you need."

"They would," Kelly agreed, "but this isn't the time to ask them. After his heart attack last year, Dad decided to take early retirement, and they need a cash reserve. So I'll have to sharpen up my typing skills and hope that estate with the wonderful house doesn't go through probate too fast.''

In her room, she got out materials for Sean, then went into her office. She got the Yellow Pages and began going down the list of temporary employment agencies. Temporary work didn't pay as well as a speech pathology position, but what choice did she have?

Then she heard a sound, looked up, and was surprised to see Grant Stuart looming in her doorway. Putting her personal concerns aside, she smiled at him. ''Come in and sit down.''

She hadn't seen him since their trip to the zoo, and she realized she'd missed him. He annoyed her, but he also intrigued and challenged her.

This morning, in his usual conservative business attire—navy suit, pale blue shirt, red and navy geometric patterned tie—he looked wonderful. Automatically, her pulse speeded up.

''Been talking to Sean?'' she asked.

To her surprise, he nodded. ''A little.''

Pleased, Kelly beamed at him. ''You're making progress.''

He gave her a boyish grin, the grin that did funny things to her insides. ''So's Sean, thanks to you.'' Then he added, ''I have a proposition for you. Sean will be at my ranch this summer—''

''But he's just beginning to talk,'' Kelly couldn't help interrupting. ''He *has* to continue through the summer.'' Her calm, professional persona deserted her, but Sean needed an advocate and she'd appointed herself. Damn Grant Stuart! Whenever she started to like him, he did something stupid. She resisted the urge to smack him and said, ''Consistency is important. He's starting to put words together, and—''

''Whoa!'' Grant held up his hand. ''That's where my proposition comes in.''

Kelly frowned, puzzled.

"I want you to work with Sean full time this summer."

"Full time?" she echoed, not sure she'd heard him correctly.

"Yes. I'd like to hire you, have you spend the summer with him at the ranch." He leaned forward and continued earnestly, "You've been good for him, I can see that."

Kelly was dazed, astonished, thrilled. Like a gift from heaven, this was the perfect solution to the problem of summer employment. But working for Grant— "I don't know," she murmured. "I—"

"I'll be in Boston most of the summer. I probably won't get home more than two or three weekends," Grant went on. "I want someone I can trust as Sean's therapist. You've made a great start. Why not keep a good thing going?"

Before Kelly could answer, he continued. "Of course, you won't have to spend the entire day with him. You can set your own schedule, and you'll have time off each week, days of your own choosing. The ranch has a pool and horses. You can think of it as a working vacation."

Still stunned, Kelly murmured, "You're very persuasive."

"When I need to be. Now, about salary." He named a figure twice what she'd counted on earning at the hospital, then rose and smiled at her. Obviously, he knew when to end the negotiation—when he had her in total shock.

"I'll . . . I'll give your offer some thought," Kelly managed.

"Sure. Take a couple of days to think it over. Give me a call Wednesday, and I'll have my secretary type up a contract." He headed for the door. "Have a nice day."

Kelly sat totally still, staring into space, then realized it was time for Sean's session. When she reached his classroom, she pulled Marla over to one side. "I have to talk to you," she whispered. "You won't believe what's happened."

"In the last fifteen minutes?"

Kelly shook her head. "Nope. In the last five."

"What?"

"I can't talk now," Kelly told her. "I'll come back at noon." She grabbed Sean's hand and left Marla staring after her with a baffled look on her face.

At twelve she hurried back and waited while Marla dismissed her class. When the children were gone, Marla said, "Let me guess. You've won the Publishers' Clearinghouse Sweepstakes and solved your money problems."

"Not quite, but you're close." While Marla organized materials for the next day, Kelly got out her sack lunch. Between bites of her sandwich, she related Grant's proposal.

Marla rolled her eyes. "You said you'd give his offer some thought? Are you nuts? What more could you want? An easy job at double the salary you'd make anywhere else. You'll have the money for the school. You'll be working with a kid you adore in great surroundings. You can go horseback riding—"

"And I could write a paper," Kelly added. " 'The Effect on Language Development of Total Immersion in an Experiential Language Stimulation Program,' or something equally dry."

"So, what are you waiting for? Call Grant and say yes."

Kelly frowned at her hands. "I'm not sure spending the summer at the ranch is the right thing to do."

Marla looked surprised. "What on earth could be wrong?"

"How would it look," Kelly asked, "my staying at Grant's house?"

"Ah," Marla said, "you're worried about your reputation."

"Yeah. You know how people talk."

Marla spread her hands. "What would they have to talk about? You said Grant's going to be in Boston all summer."

"I know, but I'd still be living there . . ."

"Kelly Connery," Marla said in an exasperated tone, "no one is going to say anything at all. Why are you so worried?"

"Reputation is important to me."

"And yours is impeccable," Marla assured her.

"Yes, but a good name can be ruined in a minute." She tore a strip off her lunch bag and began to fold it into tiny pleats.

Marla sat down beside her. "You're thinking of Nick again."

Kelly nodded. She folded another strip of paper. "He almost ruined my career. If I hadn't transferred from neurology to children's services, my professional life could have been over almost before it began."

Marla put her hand over Kelly's. "Nick was a user. And you thought you were in love with him. This situation is different."

Kelly stared at the table. "Right," she muttered.

"Uh-oh. What aren't you telling me?"

Kelly met Marla's eyes. "I have to admit I'm attracted to Grant." She wasn't willing to voice the rest—that she found him more than attractive. He was unsettling, exciting. She sensed that beneath the cool, distant facade lay a passionate, vulnerable man, a man she could care for deeply.

She wondered if Marla read all that in her eyes. But her friend simply gave her an arch look and said, "So you're afraid people will think you're actually doing what you're only fantasizing?" When Kelly nodded, Marla laughed. "Ms. Connery, this is the nineteen nineties, not the eighteen nineties. Nothing's wrong with having a relationship with a man, *especially*," she added, "when you're having it in your head. Besides, most of those people you're worried about have done the same thing. In real life.''

"People expect more of someone they entrust their children to than they do of themselves.''

"Poppycock!" Marla said. "Besides, you'll be living with Sean, not his father. Now listen to me, Kelly Connery. I'll say this in the same simple words I use with my three-year-olds—*take this job!* You're a fool if you don't.''

"Okay, okay," Kelly laughed. "I'll think about it.''

By Wednesday she'd decided Marla was right. Having the money for The Language Center and providing ongoing treatment for Sean were worth the risks involved in working for Grant. She called him and told him yes.

When she arrived at school the next day, the contract was in her box. She signed it immediately.

"Kelly Connery's on line two.''

"Thanks," Grant said. With a feeling of anticipation, he lifted the receiver. "Have you signed the contract?" he asked.

"Yes.''

Grant smiled. He hadn't realized how anxiously he'd been awaiting her assent. "Can you be at the ranch June first?''

"Mm hmm, provided I figure out what to do about Walter.''

Walter. He hadn't seen any signs of male habitation when he'd picked her up for their outing, but he'd only come to the door. Why hadn't it occurred to him that she lived with someone? "Can't Walter fend for himself this summer?" he snapped.

"I suppose. Except for mealtimes.''

What a spoiled bastard. "Can't he learn to cook?''

She chuckled. "Walter's exceptional, but he's still only a cat.''

"Oh." He felt like a fool. But he was ridiculously

relieved that Walter wasn't her lover. He cleared his throat. "Can't someone keep him for you?"

"I'll ask around." She paused a minute, then added, "I'll drop your contract in the mail this afternoon."

"No," he said quickly, "I'll come by and pick it up. We need to go over some details. How about eight tonight?"

"All right."

Grant arrived at eight sharp.

Kelly wore a pair of shorts that revealed long, shapely legs and a baggy shirt that didn't reveal as much as he'd have liked. He was still in his suit.

"Come in and make yourself comfortable," she said. "I'll take your jacket."

As she reached for the jacket, he inhaled the now familiar scent of her cologne. Apple blossoms. Suddenly he remembered visiting his grandparents in Virginia and summer evenings spent beneath their apple tree—playing, talking, dreaming. Happy times, filled with wonder and innocence.

While she went to hang up the jacket, he sat on the sofa and looked around him. The room had a country look. Pillows were piled by a small fireplace, violets grew in pots on the windowsills, a huge schefflera sat in a planter in one corner, and books and pictures were everywhere. *Relaxed*, he thought. *Warm*. Just what his home lacked. His surroundings were too formal. His *life* was too formal. He loosened his tie.

"How about some wine?" Kelly called.

"Okay."

"I hope white's all right," she said, coming in with two glasses. She handed him one, went back for a tray of cheese and crackers, and then sat down on the other end of the couch and tucked her legs under her. "You wanted to talk about the summer."

Her scent reached his nostrils again, and for a moment he forgot what he'd intended to say. He felt the stirrings of desire and shifted uncomfortably.

He cleared his throat and adopted a businesslike tone. "I assume the contract's acceptable. Two hours with Sean in the morning and two in the afternoon."

"Yes, but I'll feel free to modify the time. One day we may work all afternoon, another, thirty minutes at lunch and some time later, depending on the activities I choose."

"You're the expert. I'll leave that to your judgment. Now, what materials will you need?"

"Sean should bring his favorite toys, and I have a few things I'll bring, too. But we won't need special materials."

He'd expected a long list of supplies. "But I thought—"

"Grant, the way to teach language is through daily living. Sean'll learn while he's taking a bath or feeding the horses or helping me fix a sandwich. The best therapy is to take language out of the clinic and into the world. We'll have a golden opportunity to do that this summer."

Her face lit up and her eyes glowed when she talked about her plans. "You're . . . passionate about your work," he remarked and wondered if that passion extended to other areas as well.

Kelly shrugged. "Sometimes I get carried away. It's easy to do when you care about something. Don't you feel that way about your work?"

"I suppose," he said thoughtfully. "Building is exciting—working out the kinks, watching a development take shape, knowing you've created something useful."

"There, you see. You're just as passionate as I am."

She was right, he thought. He did care about his work, though he never put those feelings into words. Because most people wouldn't understand. Most people saw what he did as practical business at best and exploitation at worst. No one but Kelly had ever seen it as a passion. He felt a bond between them. Suddenly he wanted to know everything about her, to understand what had made her the person she was. "How did you choose this profession you feel so passionately about?" he asked.

"I like challenges."

"But why speech? You could have picked law or medicine."

"My brother had a lisp. He went to a speech clinic, and sometimes I had to go along. I was always fascinated by the speech pathologist. I never wanted to be anything else. Besides, what could be more challenging than teaching a child to communicate? Or," she added, with a mischievous smile, "teaching a parent to talk to a child?"

He grinned at the obvious reference and leaned back, letting the wine and the conversation relax him. "I'm surprised you don't want your own clinic."

"Oh, I have bigger plans than that. I want my own school." He frowned and she went on. "I plan to open a preschool for kids like Sean—kids with language problems."

"When?"

"My timetable says a year from now, thanks to you. Your salary is very generous."

He smiled, knowing she was right. But he'd wanted to make an offer she couldn't afford to turn down. "Pat will be sorry to lose you. So will the parents. They think you're a saint."

Kelly laughed. "How do you know?"

"I checked you out before I came for that first conference."

"Of course," Kelly said. "Just as you should. Some parents don't bother, but you're a sensible man."

He wondered if she'd meant that as a compliment or a sign that he was a stuffed shirt. He was tempted to ask, but a movement from the other side of the room drew his attention. A large gray cat ambled into the room. "This must be Walter," Grant remarked.

The animal stopped and stared at Grant warily, then

lowered himself to a crouch and slunk forward. When he reached the couch, he sniffed Grant's shoes, then as if satisfied that Grant was a friend, leaped into his lap.

"I'm amazed," Kelly said. "Walter hates strangers."

"Looks friendly to me," Grant said. The cat was settled in his lap, paws kneading rhythmically. Grant scratched Walter's head. "Did you find someone to take care of him for the summer?"

"He's going to board at Marla's." She reached for Grant's glass. "More wine?"

"No," he said regretfully. "I'd better go. I have to be up early." He put Walter on the couch.

Kelly got his jacket, and they walked to the door together. He had his hand on the knob when she said, "Oh, the contract. Let me get your signed copy." When she returned with it, she smiled up at him. "Here's our agreement."

Her eyes captured him, her scent swirled around him. Instead of taking the contract, he dropped his hands to her shoulders. "Why don't we seal it?" he murmured and lowered his head.

He saw her startled look, watched her eyes widen, darken, then drift closed as his lips touched hers. He kissed her slowly, gently . . . a first kiss. Though he heard the rustle of papers dropping to the floor, though he felt her breath trembling against his mouth, he resisted the urge to crush her against him. Even when she moaned softly, he kept his hands on her shoulders, his lips soft against hers. Only when he reached the edge of his control, did he let her go.

He bent and picked up the contract, then opened the door. "Good night," he murmured, went out, and shut the door behind him.

In the car, he waited for his pulse to slow, his emotions to settle. She'd called him a sensible man, but when he'd tasted her, common sense had fled. Her lips were like nectar—honeyed, sweet. One sip had given rise to a thirst that wouldn't easily be quenched. What, he wondered, had he gotten himself into?

Kelly leaned against the door. Her heart hammered in her ears, her knees trembled. She lifted an unsteady hand to her mouth and traced the imprint of Grant's lips. She could still taste him. His kiss was like wine—heady, intoxicating. And addicting. Only yesterday she'd told herself she could ignore the attraction she felt for him. How could she ignore this feeling that raged inside her? Not attraction, but need. "Oh, God," she whispered. "What have I gotten myself into?"

SIX

Kelly turned off the main highway in La Grange and down a Farm-to-Market road. Through the car window she watched large black crows circling lazily against endless blue sky. Wildflowers painted fields with swatches of pink and yellow. A gentle breeze stirred the leaves of oaks and an occasional weeping willow. Summer. She was looking forward to the next three months.

She'd convinced herself what had happened between her and Grant had been a moment's madness. By now he'd probably forgotten that impulsive kiss. As she should have. Only thing was, she hadn't. Not that it mattered. Grant had told her he'd rarely be at the ranch. So the scene wouldn't be repeated, and she should be glad. *Should* be, but she wasn't. She'd spent too many nights reliving his kiss and longing for more.

She spied the entrance to the Lazy S Ranch ahead and turned onto an unpaved drive that meandered past wide green fields until it reached a two-story gray frame house with a porch along two sides. White wicker furniture with brightly flowered upholstery was arranged on the porch, and an old-fashioned swing hung from chains beside the front door. Rosebushes and honeysuckle bordered the porch, and a huge magnolia tree shaded one side of the house. Kelly got out of her car and breathed in the mingled scents of flowers and grass.

A black and white Border collie appeared from behind the house, wagging his tail and barking. "Hi, fella," she said, as he came abreast of her.

The front door opened, and Olivia stepped out. "Sean," she called over her shoulder, "guess who's here."

As Kelly mounted the porch steps, she heard the sound of small feet running, then Sean tore outside and propelled himself into her arms. "Hi, Ke-ee," he shouted.

"Hi, hot shot," she said, giving him a hug.

"Come in and make yourself at home," Olivia said. She waved to a middle-aged man coming around the side of the house. When he reached them, she said, "This is Mr. Potter, the caretaker."

Mr. Potter shook the hand Kelly offered. "I'll bring your bags in."

"Stay out, Tex," Olivia ordered the dog, but Tex edged his way into the house, and while Sean occupied himself with the collie, Kelly took a moment to look around.

The surroundings were totally at odds with Grant's formal River Oaks home. The living room furniture was ordinary, but it was upholstered in buttery yellow, cheerful green, and woodsy brown. Pillows in matching colors were grouped before a large stone fireplace. Dried flowers in baskets, a collection of wooden decoys, a horse in bronze—all gave the room a comfortable, homey ambience. Here were the mementos that were missing from Grant's city home, family photographs arranged on a table, sports trophies lined up on a shelf.

Olivia noticed Kelly's scrutiny. "Like it?" she asked.

"Very much. But I'm also surprised," Kelly admitted. "This has a different feel from the house in Houston."

Olivia nodded. "Grant never changed anything there after Claudia died. This place now, this one's pure Grant."

Pure Grant? Kelly looked around again. She pictured Grant in a paneled study with businesslike furnishings in subdued colors, not in this cheerful room that seemed to welcome her with open arms. These surroundings reflected a man whom Kelly had barely begun to suspect existed beneath Grant's cold exterior—the person in the photograph, the man who'd kissed her with such gentle passion.

Olivia showed Kelly to her room, and she unpacked, then joined the housekeeper and Sean for lunch. Afterward, when Olivia took Sean upstairs for a nap, Kelly went into the living room and wandered over to the bookshelf. Grant's reading tastes were eclectic, everything from Texas history to poetry to best-sellers. She pulled several books from the shelf. The pages were well worn. Funny, she'd never pictured Grant relaxed enough to sit down and read. Here at his ranch, she was learning something new about him every minute.

Eager to know more, she inspected the photographs. She found one of a teenage Grant in a baseball uniform, shouldering a bat; another of him clowning with two other teenagers who looked so much like him, they had to be his sister and brother. Other pictures showed an older couple she surmised were Grant's parents, Grant with groups of friends, but she didn't see a single picture of Claudia or of Sean. Why?

She pondered this at night as she lay in her room, looking out at the star-filled sky, but she came to no conclusion. Still, her mind returned often to Grant even though she was busy with Sean. Who was Grant, really? His tragic loss seemed to have scarred him, to have covered all his emotions with a thick, impenetrable crust.

Over the next two weeks, she and Sean took advantage of the ranch's unlimited possibilities for language stimulation. They made pudding in the kitchen under Olivia's fond gaze, planted cucumbers and squash in the yard, fed the horses, explored the stable, waded in the creek. They splashed in the pool, and drawing on her experience as a camp counselor, Kelly began teaching Sean to swim. Every day he added new words to his vocabulary. Now he routinely put two and three words together.

Kelly began getting up at dawn. She would saddle one of the horses and ride through the fields with Tex trotting alongside, enjoying the colors, the fresh breeze, and the dewy grass.

On the second Friday of her stay, Kelly came back from her morning ride to find Olivia in the kitchen, compiling a grocery list. "Grant called," she explained. "he's coming in this afternoon, and he's invited company for dinner."

Grant! Kelly felt her pulse skittering in her throat. She hadn't seen him since the incident at her door, nor had she even talked to him. He'd been out of his office when she called to tell him when she'd be leaving for the ranch, so feeling she'd been given a reprieve, she'd left a message with his secretary. "I . . . I thought he wouldn't be coming in much," she said.

"Some friends are coming out to their place near here, so he thought he'd come too, long as he's going to be in Texas."

"Oh," Kelly murmured. Grant would spend some time with Sean, and the rest of the weekend he'd be occupied with his friends. She'd hardly have to see him at all except to give him a brief report of Sean's progress. She could manage that.

Although she thought she'd convinced herself, Kelly became increasingly nervous as the day wore on. She found herself looking over her shoulder at the driveway while she and Sean were at the pool and pacing the floor of her room while Sean napped.

When Grant hadn't arrived by three, she decided to take Sean to the creek. Maybe the walk would calm her nerves. She picked up a plastic bucket and toy fishing pole, and they started out.

They lay on their stomachs beside the creek and gazed at the trickling stream. Enjoying the warmth of the sun on her back and the sight of the sparkling, clear water, Kelly almost forgot Grant's impending arrival.

"Look," she whispered, pointing to a school of minnows. "See the fish."

"Baby fish?" Sean asked.

"Yes, little ones."

"Sean get 'em," the child cried and grabbed at one with a chubby fist. "Gone," he lamented, as he came up empty-handed.

"You can't catch them. The fish go fast," Kelly explained.

"Fast," Sean echoed. "Look! More fish!"

"No, that's a frog," Kelly said. "See, he's hopping."

"Frog hop!" Sean shrieked as the frog headed toward the bank. Gleefully, he scrambled after the frog, slipped, and fell in the mud. Fearing he might fall in the creek, Kelly caught him and managed to get splattered with mud herself.

Drat! She could imagine Grant driving up with his guests and finding her and his son streaked with dirt.

"Let's wash off," she suggested, and the two of them waded into the creek. Sean smacked at the water with his palms, soaking Kelly's blouse and shorts. *Better wet than dirty*, she thought. She tied her shirttail under her breasts and urged Sean out of the water, hoping to get him back to the house and into clean clothes before Grant arrived.

Sean had other ideas. "Wanna fish," he demanded, turning back to the creek as Kelly started up the bank.

"No, Sean, not now. Daddy's coming," Kelly said. "Let's go see if he's here."

"No! Fish!"

"We'll come back," Kelly promised. "Come on."

Sean planted his feet, stuck his thumb in his mouth, then took it out long enough to insist, "Gonna fish . . . now."

Kelly often found Sean's stubborn streak amusing but not now. Not when both of them were filthy and she was in a hurry. She compromised. "Okay, we'll catch one." Luckily, she'd taken the plastic bucket with her. She dipped it in the water and helped Sean scoop up half a dozen minnows. They'd make an interesting subject for conversation, and later she could dump them back in the creek. "Here're the fish. Now let's go."

Glad the driveway was still empty, she herded Sean back to the house. Setting the bucket on the hall table, she ushered the child upstairs. Twenty minutes later he was scrubbed and dressed in fresh clothes.

She had time for a shower, too, Kelly thought, but Sean announced, "Want my fish."

"Stay here. I'll get them." She could just imagine him spilling the bucket of water on the stairs.

Halfway down the stairs, she stopped. Grant came into the front hall, the screen door clattering shut behind him.

Their eyes met. She saw Grant's change from burnished pewter to obsidian as they focused on her face, then moved leisurely down her body, lingering on the damp cotton outlining her breasts, the patch of tanned skin at her midriff. Kelly felt a flush spread over her. She couldn't move, could only stare at Grant as a slow smile curved his lips.

"Kelly," he murmured. Was his voice a bit husky? *Don't be an idiot. Remember, professionalism.* She cleared her throat. "Hello, Grant. We were wondering when you'd get here. Sean's fine. I'm, uh, getting his minnows.'' She was babbling like a fool, but she couldn't seem to stop.

Grant watched her silently as she descended the rest of the stairs and grabbed Sean's bucket.

The door to the kitchen opened, and Olivia came out. ''Grant. Did you have a good trip?''

Without taking his eyes from Kelly, he answered, ''Fine.''

''How about dinner at six?''

He nodded. ''See you then, Kelly.''

''Oh, no,'' she protested. ''Sean and I will eat early and leave you to your company.''

''No,'' he said. ''Sean can eat early, but I'd like you to join us.'' She hesitated. ''Please,'' he added.

''All . . . all right.'' She turned and fled up the stairs, took the bucket into Sean's room, and left him to watch his catch.

In her room, she glanced at the mirror. Her face was flushed, her clothing damp and dishevelled. What a way to meet Grant, she thought, rubbing ineffectually at a spot of dirt on her cheek. She looked like an urchin. But this evening she'd project an air of professional competence. No frills, no flounces, she decided as she strode to the closet and chose a tailored silk shirtwaist. And no more stupid blushing.

When she finished her shower, she was surprised to hear voices from down the hall. Grant and Sean were having a conversation. Intrigued, she tiptoed to the door, opened it a crack, and listened. She heard Sean showing off his ''catch'' and Grant's approving comments. Short comments. ''Hallelujah!'' she whispered. ''You have possibilities after all, Mr. Stuart.'' With a smile of satisfaction, she shut the door and began dressing.

At six o'clock she went downstairs. By now she'd recovered her poise and greeted Grant and his guests with ease and warmth. The visitors included Grant's attorney, Sam Eldridge, and his wife Lynn, who had a ranch nearby. Two other men, Bob Harris and Adam Lawlor, and one unattached female, Lynn's sister, Tara Nolan, completed the group. Kelly couldn't help wondering, with a little twinge of jealousy, if Tara was Grant's companion for the weekend. She didn't wear a wedding ring, and she was certainly attractive. Nevertheless, except for Sam and Lynn, she couldn't determine who belonged with whom. Everyone seemed to be friendly with everyone else. Even Grant was more talkative than usual, playing the role of affable host.

Lynn sat beside Kelly. "Grant tells me you're spending the summer with Sean," she remarked. "You'll have to bring him by to play with my kids. Marianne is five, and Derek's three. He's in Sean's class at school."

"I think I know Derek," Kelly said. She'd heard Marla mention Derek, describing him as one of her brightest students. The thought that Lynn's children attended Cedar Grove made Kelly uncomfortable, since it meant Lynn knew all the other mothers. She wondered if Lynn had a wagging tongue.

Not that Kelly had kept her summer job a secret. This was a business arrangement after all. But socializing with Grant and his crowd was a different matter. That changed her from a professional to . . . what? A woman who was living in Grant Stuart's weekend retreat? She didn't want that to become the topic of gossip at Cedar Grove. Her future was too important to risk speculation about her role here. She'd have to be very careful.

"I've seen you at the school," Lynn said.

"Yes, I'm the speech pathologist. I'm here to work with Sean on language development." Better make her position very clear.

"I see. Well, do come by. The kids will enjoy playing with Sean, and I can use the company when Tara leaves."

"I'll do that." Kelly meant it. Involving Sean with

other children would help his progress, and besides, she could use some company herself.

At dinner Kelly sat between Bob and Adam. She found them both pleasant company, especially Adam, who had a wry sense of humor. Frequently though, she found Grant's brooding eyes on her, the intensity of his gaze discomfiting.

After dinner Lynn said, "Why don't we go into town and see what's going on at the Texas Tumbleweed?"

"What's that?" Tara asked.

"A real honky-tonk," answered Sam. "A country-western band, foot stompin' music. A place where you can guzzle a couple of long necks and let your hair down."

"Sounds like fun," Tara said.

"Kelly?" Adam held out a hand.

She was tempted but refused. "Thanks, but I have some notes to make, and I promised Sean a bedtime story."

Grant frowned but said nothing, and soon the laughing crowd left the house.

Kelly watched their cars disappear down the drive. Staying behind was the right decision. Even though the house seemed suddenly too quiet. Even though she wondered how she would feel dancing the two-step in Grant's arms. With a sigh, she put those thoughts aside and went up to read to Sean.

Later she wandered downstairs, browsed through a stack of compact discs, and put one on the player. Leaving the French doors open, she went out on the porch and breathed in the night air, fragrant with flowers. Above her the sky was ebony and star studded. Crickets buzzed in the trees, and a night bird twittered sweetly. Kelly shut her eyes and imagined herself in an earlier time, dressed in a long flowing gown, standing on the porch waiting for her sweetheart. The words of a love song flowed over her—something about the moon and loneliness and love. She swayed to the music, imagining herself dancing with her lover, his arms around her, his breath warm against her cheek . . .

She heard a sound behind her, turned, and opened her eyes. Grant stood silhouetted in the doorway. For a moment, she thought he was part of her dream, then he stepped forward.

"Wh . . . what are you doing here?" she asked breathlessly. "I thought you went with the others."

"I did, but I wasn't in the mood for the Tumbleweed." He crossed the porch and stood gazing down at her. Kelly felt her heart begin a slow, deep cadence. She averted her eyes and stared across the lawn.

"Is Sean asleep?" Grant asked

"Yes."

"He's talking more."

"A lot more. You've been talking more, too. To Sean, I mean."

Grant chuckled. "I know what you mean. You've been good for Sean, Kelly. Is the schedule you've set working out?"

She nodded.

"Are you taking some time for yourself?"

"Yes. I've been riding and swimming, and I've explored La Grange."

"Good," he said. "You need time away from Sean. You should have come with us this evening."

Kelly shifted uncomfortably. "Dancing? No, I couldn't."

"Why not?" He frowned down at her.

She knew she would sound stuffy, but she needed to clarify her position. "You hired me as a professional. Going dancing with you and your friends isn't my role here."

He laughed and held out his hand. "Then dance with me now."

Kelly raised her eyes to his. Mesmerized, she stared into their gray depths. Behind her, the music swelled to a crescendo. Around her, the night breeze stirred the trees. Before her, Grant stood, waiting.

She took a step forward. The thought flashed in her mind that, with one more step, she'd never be able to go back. Still, she took the step. And moved into Grant's arms.

One of his hands closed around hers, the other touched her back. He rested his cheek against her hair and moved to the slow, sensuous beat of the music. If she closed her eyes, she could imagine she was back in the dreamworld she'd created moments ago. But reality outshone her dream. His scent, mixed with the fragrance of honeysuckle, engulfed her. His body was warm, pulsing with life, with promise. He tucked their hands between their bodies, and she could feel the thudding of his heart, mirroring the rhythm of her own.

The song ended, another began, and he dropped his hands to her waist. Automatically, she raised hers to his shoulders. She laid her cheek against his chest and drank him in, absorbed him. He pulled her closer; she tightened her arms about his neck. The music swirled, their bodies kept time. Until Kelly realized the last song had ended.

She lifted her head and looked up at Grant. "The music stopped," she whispered.

"Did it?" he asked, still holding her, still swaying. "Funny, I still hear it."

"So do I."

She couldn't tear her eyes from his. Her lips parted. His lowered. Their mouths met, and Kelly felt the earth tilt.

Their first kiss had been a tentative exploration; this one was hot demand. He took her mouth; he possessed it. His tongue invaded, captured, and hers was its willing prisoner.

His arms crushed her against him, his hands roamed over her shoulders and back. Needs rocketed through her—needs, demands, desires she hadn't even known she had. Desperate to touch, she pulled his shirt from his waistband and spread her hands over his back, feeling the smooth, warm skin, the taut muscles.

His mouth left hers, found a spot between her chin and jaw, and lingered. She'd never known one small area of skin could be so sensitive. His lips and tongue ignited an electric charge that danced through her entire body. Her knees went weak. She clung to him and whispered his name.

She heard him rasp her name, listened to his ragged breathing, then felt the heat of his hands as he unbuttoned her dress and bent his head to the hollow between her breasts. "Kelly, for God's sake, come upstairs."

Upstairs. The word registered in her brain. Upstairs to his bed. Upstairs where Sean was sleeping. What were they doing? What was she thinking?

With all her strength she shoved against his chest. "No!"

He stared at her, his eyes glazed, his breath coming in short gasps. "Kelly—"

She stepped back, clutching the crumpled fabric of her dress, feeling the night breeze, cool against her fevered skin. Desire and despair warred inside her. "No," she repeated. "We . . . I . . . can't."

He reached out, and she saw that his hand trembled. Before he could touch her, she turned and ran into the house and up the stairs.

Grant leaned against the kitchen counter, took another gulp of coffee, and grimaced. Bitter. As bitter as his mood. But then he'd never been good at making coffee. Or at judging women—his marriage had proved that. And now there was Kelly. So sweet, so warm, and then suddenly so cold.

She'd run inside as if the devil were at her heels. Why? He'd thought she wanted him. God knows, he'd wanted her. Wanted with an intensity he'd never felt before, an intensity that hadn't lessened for hours.

When she'd disappeared up the stairs, he'd dropped onto a chair and sat, his head in his hands. He forced himself to take slow even breaths, to slow the pulse pounding in his throat. His body had cooled, but his emotions hadn't. The need to touch and be touched, the need for another human being—the need for Kelly—had remained.

He went up and tried to sleep, but he couldn't. After tossing in his bed for more than an hour, he got up, pulled on an old pair of jeans, and went outside. He might have walked for miles, he didn't know. He only knew that he thought endlessly about Kelly and finally came to a conclusion. He didn't know her well, but he knew she was honest. Something had frightened her, something about the situation or about him. They needed to talk about it. He wasn't much for talking, but in this case it was necessary. Calmer after making that decision, he went back to bed and managed to sleep the rest of the night.

As always, he'd risen early, come downstairs, and ended up brooding over a cup of bitter coffee.

He heard a sound and turned as Kelly came in. She obviously hadn't expected to see him because she made a sound of dismay and put her hand to her mouth. Then she straightened and said stiffly, "I was looking for Olivia. I'm going to take my day off, and I wanted to let her know."

Her night had been as restless as his, Grant thought, noting the dark circles under her eyes. "Running away?" he asked.

Her eyes narrowed, and she squared her shoulders. "Of course not. My contract says two days off a week." Her voice was cool, professional. "I'll be back late this afternoon. That will give you a chance to spend some time alone with Sean." She moved toward the door, hesitated, and turned back to him. "Grant," she said, "last night was a . . . a mistake."

That hurt. "Was it?" To his way of thinking, last

night had been anything but. It had been joy, passion, life. No, certainly not a mistake.

But she nodded. "A mistake that won't happen again."

"Why, Kelly?" He took a step forward.

She stepped back. "It can't, that's all. What happened was unprofessional."

"You're right," he answered softly, deliberately. "It wasn't professional; it was personal." He moved closer and watched her eyes grow wide with fear, saw her hands come up as if to protect herself. He frowned. "What's wrong, Kelly? Are you afraid of me?"

"No," she said. "I'm not afraid of you." She balled her hands into fists, then abruptly turned back to the door. "I'm afraid of myself." Before he could say anything, before he could stop her, she ran out of the room.

Kelly half expected Grant to follow her when she left the kitchen, but he didn't.

His taunt reverberated in her mind. She made herself slow down and walk to her car. If he happened to look out the kitchen window, she wouldn't let him see her running away even though she knew he was right. She *was* running. As fast as she could, she admitted, getting into her car and starting the engine.

She'd wanted Grant last night with a fierce urgency that didn't dissipate as she lay sleepless in her bed. She imagined another outcome to the evening, imagined him sweeping her into his arms and carrying her up the stairs. Imagined them together in his bed, making love through the night.

She was a fool, she thought, stomping down on the accelerator. The car shot forward, and she immediately eased up on the pressure. She wasn't a foolhardy driver, nor would she be foolhardy in love. Nick had been her only serious indiscretion, and she wasn't going to repeat that mistake. Not now, when the stakes were so much higher. She had a future to think of, and she wouldn't jeopardize it by ruining her reputation. More important, she wouldn't risk her heart. She had an intuitive feeling that an affair with Grant would leave her bruised and bleeding in a way the episode with Nick had not.

She drove to Austin, where she spent the day browsing in the LBJ Library, strolling across the University of Texas campus, exploring the roads that curved along the lake west of town. Always, Grant was on her mind—the imprint of his kisses still on her lips, the sound of his voice as he'd whispered her name echoing in her ears.

Should she quit the job? Leave the ranch and go back to Houston? But, to what? To a temporary office job at much lower pay than she was earning now. No, that wouldn't do. Besides, she'd signed a contract, and she was certain Grant wouldn't let her out of it. He'd expect her to fulfill her obligation.

And she had Sean to think of. He was making such progress. How could she abandon him? Whatever her problems with his father, she'd made a commitment to the child, not only with a contract but with her heart. She loved him.

So she'd stay and hope that Grant would keep away. After all, hadn't he told her he'd be in Boston most of the summer? He probably wouldn't show up again until August. By then, both their memories of last night's fiasco would have faded.

By midweek Kelly had convinced herself that was true. She and Sean fell into their customary routine. Olivia heard nothing about Grant returning to the ranch. Everything went on just as it should.

On Thursday Lynn Eldridge invited Kelly to bring Sean over for lunch. While the children romped in the yard, she and Lynn sat on the patio with glasses of frosty mint-flavored tea. Kelly was pleased at how well Sean communicated with the two other children. Although his verbal skills weren't yet up to theirs, he could make his wants known and no longer resorted to physical means to get his messages across.

"You'll have to bring Sean over again," Lynn said.

"And plan to go to the Fourth of July celebration with us. The town puts on a real old-fashioned Fourth—parade, picnic, music, a watermelon seed–spitting contest—everything.

"Do you spend the whole summer here?" Kelly asked.

"Yes, we—" Lynn leaned forward. "Marianne, don't pull the cat's tail. You'll hurt her." She settled back and said, "Where were we? Oh, yes, the summer. Tomorrow I'm going to San Antonio to spend some time with my folks and take the kids to Sea World, but I'll be here the rest of the time. I love being in the country, and Sam comes out most weekends. What about you?"

"I'll be here until the end of August."

"That's good." Lynn took a sip of her tea. "I hope Grant will come out often."

I hope not. "I don't expect him," she told Lynn. "He plans to be in Boston most of the summer."

"Too bad. You should try to talk him into coming down. He needs to relax."

"I don't imagine I'd have much clout with him. After all, I'm just working for him," Kelly said, taking the opportunity to remind Lynn her relationship with Grant wasn't a personal one. "He seems so driven," she added.

"Yes," Lynn agreed. "It's too bad he doesn't have time to take advantage of the ranch. He loves it so much. Even during the Claudia years he used to come down occasionally, just to—" She broke off again. "Derek, get off the fence. You heard me." She half rose from her chair, nodded when the child backed away from the fence, then sat down. "Claudia was a city person," she went on. "She came here once, then never again. Country living wasn't her style."

Kelly recalled Olivia's saying the ranch house was "pure Grant." "I'm surprised Claudia didn't like the ranch," she said. "It's a great place to relax."

"Relaxing wasn't Claudia's thing," Lynn said. "She was always on the go. Always looking for glamour and excitement."

Lynn's voice had a hard edge as she talked about Grant's wife. Kelly was surprised. She'd assumed Grant's good friends had been as fond of his wife as they were of him. She wanted to know more, even though she told herself that details of Grant's marriage were none of her business.

But Lynn seemed eager to drop the topic of Claudia Stuart. "Maybe one day we can drive into Austin with the kids," she said. Then she turned to Marianne, who had trotted over with Derek and Sean in tow. "Yes, honey?"

"Mommy, can Sean spend the night?" Marianne inquired.

"I don't know, sweetie. Let's ask Kelly."

Kelly debated as four pairs of eyes turned to her. "I'd have to ask Sean's daddy about that, and he's not here." When all three children's faces fell, she added, "But I'll talk it over with him and maybe Sean can come another night."

"Aww," came a chorus of small voices.

"Can he come tomorrow?" Derek suggested.

"Tomorrow afternoon we're going to San Antonio, remember?" Lynn said.

"When we get back then?" Marianne asked.

"Kelly will check, and if Sean's daddy says yes, we'll plan on a week from Thursday. Okay with everyone?"

"Yaay! Okay!"

"Is that all right with you, Kelly?" Lynn asked when the children had gone back to their play.

Kelly nodded. "I'm sure Grant won't mind. I just feel I have to talk to him about it first."

"I understand."

Kelly sighed inwardly. She was delighted Sean was making friends but sorry she'd be forced to call Grant to get his okay for the overnight. To her way of thinking, the less contact she had with him, the better.

She and Sean got home too late for her to call. The next morning she picked up the receiver and stared at it irresolutely. Perhaps she'd make a unilateral decision. Olivia had seemed pleased at the idea of Sean's spending the night at the Eldridges'. Maybe she didn't have to discuss it with Grant at all. "Coward," she muttered to herself and placed the call.

He wasn't in. She left a message, but he didn't call back. Much as she wanted to avoid talking to him, that annoyed her. Oh well, she'd just call him Monday morning.

Saturday she put Grant out of her mind. She took Sean to a pet shop she'd discovered in La Grange, and they bought a tank and half a dozen fish. They spent a quiet afternoon watching the fish, coloring fish pictures, and putting puzzles together.

That night Kelly put Sean to bed, showered, and curled up in the rocking chair with a book. She read until she was sleepy, then got into bed.

She'd just dozed off when she heard a sound. She sat up and strained her ears. Someone had opened the front door. Perhaps Olivia was going out for a moonlit stroll. But Kelly heard heavy footsteps on the stairs. Masculine footsteps. Grant!

She lay still and listened as the footsteps moved down the hall, paused for a moment before her door, then continued. The door to Grant's room opened and closed. He was here.

The tempo of her heart increased. A warm flush spread over her body. Instead of a thousand miles away, he was a few feet from her door. This was a situation she hadn't expected to deal with, didn't want to deal with.

She heard Grant's door open, heard his step in the hall again, and then listened as the bathroom door shut and the shower went on. She imagined him nude beneath the spray, water droplets glistening on his skin. She pictured his hands moving over his chest and thighs as he bathed and was abashed to feel a gush of warmth and wetness in the lower part of her body. Dear God, if just thinking of him made her feel this way, what would happen when she met him face to face?

She'd avoid him. She could write a brief report of Sean's progress to date, put it on the table, and take another day off.

"Running away?" She repeated Grant's words. No! She wouldn't let him affect her this way. She'd handle this professionally, pretend nothing had happened between them. She'd regard this as a challenge, consider Grant a difficult parent. *Sure, Kelly.*

Sleep was slow in coming, and when she drifted off, she was plagued by disquieting dreams. Not that they were unpleasant. Her night was filled with erotic fantasies of herself and Grant, naked in each other's arms.

When she woke, far earlier than usual, she was anything but rested. Tired and tense, she needed exercise, preferably away from the house. She'd saddle one of the horses and go for a ride. Watching the sunrise as she rode across the fields would settle her nerves.

She got out of bed, slipped into a pair of jeans and an old plaid shirt, and headed for the stable, feeling better already as the cool morning air caressed her skin.

Inside the stable, the odors of horses and leather filled her nostrils. She stood still for a moment, allowing her eyes to adjust to the shadowy interior, then started toward the stall of her favorite mare. She was halfway there when she heard someone moving in one of the stalls. Mr. Potter must be feeding the horses. "Morning," she called.

"Morning." The voice wasn't Mr. Potter's.

Kelly froze as Grant stepped out of the stall and blocked her path—tall, formidable, and impossibly appealing. His shirt was open to the waist, and she could see beads of sweat gleaming on a chest forested with dark, curly hair. His sleeves were rolled up to the elbows, revealing tanned, muscular forearms. And his jeans! They hugged his lower body like a lover. Kelly's mouth went dry. "Wh . . . what are you doing here?" she croaked.

His lips curved in a slow, sensuous smile. "Feeding the horses."

"No, I . . . I mean, what are you doing at the ranch?"

"Spending the weekend," he said, giving her another of those infuriating smiles.

"But you said you wouldn't be in. You're supposed to be in Boston all summer." In her own ears, her voice sounded petulant.

"I changed my mind," Grant said, moving closer.

Kelly glanced over her shoulder, looking for an escape route. The door seemed miles away. And Grant was so close. Near enough for her to feel the heat of his body, hear the whisper of his breath. "B . . . business in Texas?" she asked, trying to sound casual and knowing she'd failed miserably.

"Unfinished business." He reached out and caught her hand, his grip firm.

Kelly tried to pull away and found herself backed up against the wall. "Don't run away from me, Kelly," he murmured. "Not this time."

With his arms boxing her in, she had nowhere to run, nowhere to hide.

"I thought of you all week." He brushed his hand across her cheek. Kelly felt a quiver run through her body. His hand moved to her throat. "Your skin is so soft."

She should stop this now. But she seemed to have lost her ability to speak, to move. She stood, spellbound, as his mouth came closer. "I want you, Kelly," he whispered. "Say you want me, too."

She stared into his eyes and saw not the steely determination of the businessman, but longing, need.

Suddenly she didn't want to run. The man before her was open, vulnerable. She didn't know why, but something in her ached to reach out to him. All at once, the same love she felt for his child welled up in her heart and spilled over to the father. She put her arms around his neck. "I want you, too," she said and drew his mouth down to hers.

Their lips met, fused. His body pressed against hers, warm, strong, and as familiar as if she'd always known him, as if she'd felt him against her a thousand times. She didn't know why that should be, didn't care. All that mattered was the feel of him, the nearness.

With lips and hands, they aroused one another. She ran her hands over his back, laid her cheek against the springy curls on his chest, then searched for his small, tight nipples and caressed them with her tongue.

He found the spot on her jaw he'd kissed last week and nibbled at it, his lips and tongue teasing until she cried out. He peeled away her shirt and kissed his way down to her breasts, then freed them from her bra and pressed his lips to one throbbing peak.

"Come with me," he breathed, taking her arm.

Kelly glanced toward the door, then looked down at her state of undress. "We . . . we can't go out."

"Here." He led her to an open stall, piled with hay, then pulled her back into his arms. "Kelly," he whispered, running his fingers through her tangle of curls, kissing her forehead, her eyelids. She urged his mouth back to hers, drinking in the heady taste of him, more intoxicating than the finest wine.

His kisses became urgent, his hands rushed over her. He stripped off her jeans and his, took off his shirt and spread it out, then lowered her to the hay.

Somewhere in her head she could hear the music they'd danced to, the lyrics that spoke of unending love. She felt the softness of Grant's shirt beneath her and the prickly hay the shirt didn't quite cover. She breathed in the sweet clover smell and knew the most luxurious bed couldn't compare. She was here with Grant, and she wanted to give him everything. She wanted to warm his heart and his body, fill the empty spaces in his life.

And then he came inside her, filling her, too. Filling an emptiness she didn't even know existed. Until now.

Everything disappeared. She was no longer conscious of the stable, no longer aware of anything but Grant—the movements of his body, the thunder of his heart, the feel of his skin.

Together they set a rhythm as old as time. Together they spiraled upward and rocketed into space, and together they held each other as they slowly settled to earth.

They lay silently, wrapped in each other's arms. Sanity returned, and with it, doubts. What had happened to her firm resolve not to become involved with Grant? Where were "Connery's Commandments"? Broken, shattered. And what now? Kelly lifted her head. "Grant, I—"

"Sh." He put his finger on her lips. "Don't say anything to spoil it."

She laid her head back and turned so she could see his eyes. "I wasn't planning on this—"

"This?" he asked, leaning over her to circle her ear with his tongue. "Or this?" He brushed his fingers over her nipple. Immediately it tightened. "You're so responsive," he murmured, bending over to take the peak in his mouth. She whimpered, and he chuckled. "I've heard that sound in my dreams all week."

He continued to tease her nipple with his tongue until a thought occurred to her, and she wriggled away, stood up, and began searching for her clothes. "Grant! Mr. Potter—"

"—has the morning off," he said complacently.

"Did you plan this?" she demanded as she pulled on her jeans.

"No," he laughed. "How could I have known you'd appear just when I wanted you? But if I had staged it, I couldn't have picked a better spot for our first time." When she started to interrupt, he stopped her. "And it *is* just the first. This wasn't just a roll in the hay, Kelly. For either of us."

Silently, they stared at one another. Kelly nodded, and they continued to dress. When they stepped out of the stall, Grant said, "I have to finish with the horses. I'll be back after a while, and we can talk about Sean." He brushed a stalk of hay from her hair.

"Yes, about Sean." She'd almost forgotten why she was here.

She left Grant in the stable and walked back to the house. She had been thoroughly loved. She was exhilarated. She was confused. Not about her feelings for Grant. She was as sure of them as she was that the sun would come up tomorrow. But she was uncertain of his feelings for her. He'd intimated something, but what? His definition of "more than a roll in the hay" might not match hers. And she was uncomfortable with their situation now that she'd done what she'd sworn she'd never do: gotten involved with a client. And she had to consider Sean as well. A totally confusing picture.

Foregoing breakfast, she went upstairs, brushed her hair, and straightened her clothing. Then she returned to the kitchen, where Sean was finishing his cereal.

Kelly tried to keep the morning routine, to pretend that nothing unusual had happened, but that was hard when Grant appeared. Whenever their eyes met, his mouth curved into a satisfied half-smile, his eyes gleamed, and she knew what he was thinking. Because her thoughts were moving along the same lines.

Grant viewed the new fish, listened to Sean chatter about them, and tried to mimic Kelly's mode of talking to the child. Both father and son were making progress.

"Lynn Eldridge's kids invited Sean to spend next Thursday night," Kelly said. "Is that okay?"

"Sounds fine. I'll be in Friday."

"You'll be back so soon?" Kelly asked.

"Not soon enough," Grant murmured, then stood up. "I have to get back to Houston right away. I have some 'other' business to attend to." When Kelly's face heated, he grinned.

He hesitated, then gave Sean a quick hug. Kelly noticed that he'd even seemed less uncomfortable interacting with the child. Perhaps her early assumption that Grant would come around when Sean became more communicative was right.

"Walk me to the door," he told her. She did and stood inside as he opened the screen. "I'll see you Friday," he said. "Six days. Much too long."

He had a way of robbing her of breath. Wordlessly she nodded.

He started across the porch, then came back to her. Almost tentatively, he put out his hand and touched her cheek. "Think of me," he said, then turned and left.

EIGHT

He thought of her. All week as he sat in meetings, toured the construction site, planned, negotiated, or signed contracts, Kelly was on his mind. Her voice, her smile, the way he'd felt inside her.

How long since he'd known this hunger? This pure desire for another human being? He'd spent time with women since Claudia had died. A few of them, he'd slept with—he couldn't call it making love. It had been more of a physical release, on both sides. But what he felt for Kelly was different. Deeper, more intense. He wanted to know her, not just in the physical sense but in every possible way a man could know a woman.

On Friday he concluded his work with unusual haste, made a plane reservation for twelve o'clock instead of the afternoon flight he normally booked, and left his office without a backward glance.

To his disgust, his plane was delayed at the Dallas–Fort Worth airport, and it was late afternoon by the time he arrived at Houston Intercontinental and picked up his car. Then, rush hour added more frustration. Outbound traffic, always sluggish on weekends, seemed hellish today. Because he had something to look forward to—some*one* to look forward to. Kelly.

When he arrived at the ranch, a sense of peace replaced his irritation. Dusk softened the outlines of the house. The downstairs windows were dark, but on the second floor a light glowed in Sean's room. As if the light were a beacon, Grant started toward it. He took the porch steps two at a time, dropped his bag in the hall, and climbed the stairs.

When he reached the top and turned down the hall, he heard Kelly's voice, then Sean's. He stopped just outside Sean's door and watched them.

They sat on the bed, leaning against the pillows. Kelly held a book propped against her knees. She had one arm around Sean, cuddling him against her shoulder. Lamplight fell softly across her face, highlighting the rich red-blond of her hair.

Sean, in baseball pajamas, hair damp and curly, his teddy bear in his arms, pointed to the book. "Big chair," he said.

"Yes, that's Daddy Bear's chair. It's very big," she said in a deep, father-bear voice. She turned the page. "Here's—"

"Mama Bear's chair," Grant said from the doorway.

Kelly's head jerked up. "Grant!"

"Daddy!" Sean cried and scrambled down from the bed.

As he picked up his son and hugged him, Grant felt an ineffable sorrow that his marriage had been so empty. Even if Claudia had lived, he'd never have caught her sitting on the bed reading a fairy tale to her child . . . and enjoying herself.

He hugged Sean tight, and in a moment, the sadness was gone. Claudia was yesterday; Sean was today. Sean and Kelly. He smiled at her over the child's head and saw her cheeks flush.

"Kelly reading bears," Sean said as Grant set him down.

"Maybe Daddy would like to read you the rest,"

Kelly suggested, getting up and offering the book to Grant.

Claudia would not have read Sean a bedtime story, but Grant realized he'd never done so either. Ashamed he'd neglected his son for so long, he sat beside Sean. "Mama Bear had a middle-sized chair," he began. Sean was instantly enthralled, and Grant felt his guilt ease. Perhaps he could make up for lost time.

"I'll let you two enjoy the story," Kelly said and left.

She paused in the doorway for a moment, looking at father and son. Their heads, one dark, one fair, were bent over the pages. As she watched, Grant put his arm around Sean's shoulders and pulled him close. Listening to the rumble of Grant's voice and breathing a prayer of thanks that he had begun reaching out to his child, she went downstairs.

Olivia came out of the kitchen. "Did I hear the front door open just now?"

"Grant came in a few minutes ago. He's upstairs reading Sean a story."

Their eyes met for a long moment, and Olivia wiped a tear from her cheek. Kelly nodded at the older woman in perfect understanding, then said, "I'm going for a walk."

Outside, she strolled across the lawn and down the road toward the creek with Tex at her heels. Violet shadows surrounded her, and the sweet smell of summer grass drifted to her nostrils. She picked a pale yellow buttercup and walked on, twirling it in her hand.

She glanced over her shoulder at the light in Sean's room. Now that Grant had returned to the ranch, what would happen between them? They couldn't go back, yet the future was uncertain.

She walked down the winding road, stopping beneath the spreading canopy of a weeping willow. She stood beneath the tree and watched a sliver of moon appear in the sky. She waited.

Grant came to her. He drew her into his arms, kissed her with a patient thoroughness that left her weak, then pulled her head against his shoulder and whispered, "I've missed you."

"I've missed you, too."

"Did you think of me?"

"Yes," she admitted. "More than I wanted to. More than was wise."

He drew back and looked into her eyes. His brow furrowed. "Why do you say that?"

"We had a professional relationship. What happened last week changed that."

"I certainly hope so."

Kelly shook her head. "I've been careful to keep our association therapist and client, no matter . . . no matter how I felt."

"I haven't thought of us as client-therapist for a long time," Grant murmured. He took his lips on a lazy journey from her temple down her cheek. "You haven't either."

"No," Kelly said, "but I've tried not to let my feelings get mixed up with my work."

"You have feelings for Sean."

He kissed her throat, the curve of her shoulder, and Kelly couldn't prevent a quiver of pleasure. "Those are different. They're acceptable."

She saw the hurt in Grant's eyes as he said, "And your feelings for me aren't?"

She took a step back and put her hands on his chest to prevent him from pulling her closer. "I got involved once at work. It was a disaster."

She moved away, but he reached for her hand and turned her toward him. "Tell me about it."

"Let's walk," she suggested, and they left the shelter of the tree. Kelly was silent as they wandered toward the creek. Finally, she took a breath and began. "I met Nick soon after I started my internship at St. Stephen's Hospital. I was assigned to the rehab clinic, and he was a neurologist. At first, we talked, joked around, sometimes had lunch in the hospital cafeteria. Then he asked me out.

"Nick was charming, funny, intelligent, and we had common interests. What could be more perfect? We became involved . . . seriously involved, I thought. Then—"

She paused. The only sound was the chirp of crickets and, as they neared the creek, the croak of a frog.

"Then?" Grant prodded.

"Then he asked me to add several patients to my caseload. I said I'd give their names to the rehab director, but Nick said no. He wanted to see them. I was flattered, of course. I tested all three of them. I didn't have much experience then, but I had enough to know that none of them could benefit from speech therapy."

"Wouldn't a doctor have known that?" Grant asked.

"Sure, but some doctors get a cut for referring patients who are on their service."

"I see. What happened?"

"I told Nick when he came over that evening that none of those patients could profit from therapy. He was furious. He wanted those people on the rolls, no questions asked. All of a sudden, he became someone else, someone I didn't know. He told me I was inexperienced, naive about how a hospital service worked . . . and a lot of other things. Then he stalked out of my apartment and slammed the door. The next day he went to the clinic director and told him I was incompetent, insubordinate."

"That must have hurt."

"Yes, but I was still foolish enough to see Nick the man and Nick the doctor as separate. After a ten-minute conversation I realized they were one and the same. I went to his office to talk to him, told him what we had together was important, that I didn't want to see it ruined because of a professional disagreement. He said in the coldest voice I'd ever heard that we had nothing together. The next day at lunch I saw him dazzling the other speech pathology intern with his charm. By the end of the week, the intern and Nick were seeing one another, those three patients were on her caseload, and I had asked for a transfer to the children's unit.''

They reached the creek, and Kelly stepped past Grant, then stared at the water. After all this time, talking about how Nick had treated her still hurt.

Grant put his hands on her shoulders and pulled her back to lean against him. "He was a bastard," he said, his voice harsh. "And a user."

Kelly nodded. "But he taught me never to get my personal and professional lives mixed up. I haven't, until now."

He turned her toward him and put his hand under her chin so she met his eyes. "I won't hurt you, Kelly," he said. Then he pulled her close and kissed her with care and tenderness.

Oh, Grant. You don't know what you may do, she thought, but she stayed in his arms because she knew, no matter what might happen in the future, this was where she wanted to be.

"Come inside," Grant said, taking her hand. "I want you. In my bed, this time."

As he led her back along the path, he said, "I spent all week remembering Sunday and looking forward to tonight."

"So did I," Kelly admitted. "Sunday was like a roller coaster ride, wild and exciting."

Grant threw back his head and laughed. "I've been called many things in my life, but I've never been compared to an amusement park ride." He stopped to hug her, lifting her off her feet. "You're wonderful, Kelly. You make me feel happy."

"You need to be happy."

They walked the rest of the way in silence, through the gentle night, then across the quiet entry hall and up to Grant's room. There he took her hands. "Make me happy. Let me make you happy, too."

"Yes," she whispered and put her arms around his neck.

"No roller coaster ride this time," he murmured. "We'll take it slow and sweet."

And they did. They undressed one another in the moonlight, touching, tasting, learning the curves and angles of each other's bodies, the sounds of each other's sighs. On the bed he held her close, stroking with hands and tongue, lingering over her breasts, trailing his lips along her thigh. He was slow, he was thorough, but above all he was gentle. He made her feel cherished, as if every kiss he gave her were a precious gift.

When he entered her in a smooth, fluid motion, she was complete. She'd found her other half. No matter what happened between them, he was a part of her forever. Afterward, as he held her, she memorized his every heartbeat, every breath.

When she shifted, preparing to sit up, Grant tightened his hold. "Don't leave."

"I have to. I can't stay here all night. Sean gets up early, and sometimes he comes looking for me. I have to go."

He sighed. "You're right, of course."

She bent to kiss him and he pulled her close. "Once more," he whispered, and without hesitation she went back into his arms.

They spent the next morning lounging around the pool, that is, as much lounging as Sean would allow. He splattered them with water, insisted on jumping into the pool at two-minute intervals, and kept up a running chatter, much to Kelly's delight. At last Kelly took him into the water and let him demonstrate his dog paddle for Grant.

"I didn't expect him to swim so well," Grant remarked. "He's taken to the water like a dolphin."

Kelly agreed. "He's fearless."

"Later today I'll bring him back out and give him a lesson."

No words could form around the lump in Kelly's throat. She wondered if Grant realized this was the first time he'd volunteered to do something with Sean without her coercion.

He kept his promise. That afternoon after Sean's nap and some quiet play, they went to the pool for a swimming lesson. Kelly stayed away, giving Grant time alone with Sean.

Apparently the hour was a success. When he brought Sean inside, he said, "I can't believe what you've accomplished. He can actually carry on a conversation."

Kelly nodded. "He's learning something new every day."

"You've done wonders with him."

She shook her head. "I'll take some credit, but a lot of his progress is due to Sean himself. He's bright and motivated. All he needed was a start, and then he took over."

"But you knew how to give him that start."

That evening they took Sean to the Dairy Queen in town. Grant eyed the menu posted over the counter. "No filet mignon. No lobster."

" 'Fraid not. You'll have to make do with a hamburger," Kelly told him. "What do you want, Sean?"

"Ketchup."

Kelly stood back to see how Grant would handle this.

"Ketchup with your hamburger?" he asked.

"Huh-uh. Ketchup."

"Sean, you can't just eat ketchup."

"Sure can."

"How about a nice cheeseburger . . . or a hot dog?"

The child shook his head vehemently.

Beginning to look exasperated, Grant turned to Kelly. "Help!" he whispered out of the corner of his mouth.

She squatted beside Sean and said, "Know what? You could paint something with the ketchup." The child eyed her skeptically. "You could paint your hamburger bun." A glimmer of interest appeared in Sean's eyes. "You could dip french fries in the ketchup and watch them turn red," she continued.

"O—kay."

"Good. Tell Daddy you want a hamburger and french fries with your ketchup." As the child complied, Kelly decided that, though Grant had made progress, he still had some learning ahead about living with a young child.

They collected their order, and Grant chose a booth in the back, as far as possible from a rowdy group of teenagers and several noisy families. Kelly enjoyed the blaring jukebox, the family atmosphere of the small restaurant. Here she could pretend for a while that she and Grant and Sean belonged together.

Later, after Sean was asleep, Grant led Kelly into his room, and they made love with passionate enthusiasm. Leaving him afterward was difficult, but Kelly was adamant. Sean would not find her in his father's bed.

Before Grant left the next morning, he pulled Kelly aside for a long, ardent kiss. "I'll see you Friday," he said when they parted.

"You'll be back next week?"

He nodded. "And every time I can."

Monday night Grant called. "Sean's grandparents are back in Houston. They want to drive out tomorrow for a visit." He sounded strained.

"Fine," Kelly said. They talked a few minutes longer, then she hung up, wondering, as she had last month, about Grant's relationship with his late wife's parents.

The Hamiltons arrived at ten. Sean clung to Kelly, peering around her legs at his grandparents. Finally Joe reached into a plastic bag and brought out a Ninja Turtle figure.

"Look, Sean. It's Michelangelo, your favorite," Kelly said.

"An-jo!" Sean shrieked, and when the other three turtles appeared as well, he was hooked.

Joe sat on the floor beside Sean, and the two spent half an hour racing the turtles through imaginary sewers, serving them imaginary pizza, and helping them conquer imaginary foes.

Kelly was delighted to see Sean verbalizing and enjoying the attention from his grandfather. Listening to Joe's easy use of "Cowabunga" and "Hey, dudes," the staples of Turtle conversation, Kelly remarked to Nancy, "I'm surprised Joe is up on the latest preschool craze."

"He had to learn fast," Nancy replied. "Sean is our only grandchild. Joe's partner has four and he briefed us."

Kelly suggested they leave Joe and Sean to their play and have a cup of coffee.

"Tell me how you and Sean spend your days," Nancy said as she stirred cream into her cup. "Do you have sessions morning and afternoon?"

Kelly shook her head. "Life is our session. Whatever we do is language therapy. For instance, I've been promising Sean we'd make cookies. I thought we'd do that now and you could see how we work together."

"That would be marvelous," Nancy said, "if we can drag those two away from those outrageous turtles."

"Cookies should do it." They returned to the living room, and Kelly reminded Sean of their plans. "Let's show what good cooks we are."

"Okay. C'mon," Sean told his grandfather.

They gathered around the kitchen table, and Kelly brought out a mixing bowl, spoons, peanut butter, marshmallow creme, and vanilla wafers. "We're going to put peanut butter in the cookies," she said, opening the jar. "Want to smell?"

Everyone took turns sniffing, then Kelly dipped in the spoon and put a dab on Sean's finger. "How's it feel?"

"Sticky," he said. "Peanut butter sticky. I eat it?"

"Sure," Kelly said and watched Sean lick his finger.

"Grandma eat, too," the child said.

Nancy wrinkled her nose but extended a finger. Kelly put a tiny dab on and Nancy licked it. "Mmm!"

"Grandpa, too," Sean said, and Joe followed suit.

They counted out four tablespoonfuls, then added an equal amount of marshmallow creme. Kelly wiped a white smear from Sean's nose and another from his cheek.

"Grandma's face dirty. Got stuff on," Sean remarked.

Kelly suppressed a laugh at Nancy's grimace, but the older woman chuckled and said, "Help me clean it, Sean."

Kelly smiled as Sean helped Nancy dampen a paper towel and sponge her cheek. All the while, Nancy fed him short sentences, and Sean responded. Would Grant have done that? Would he have even thought of it? Not likely. Grant was making progress, but he lacked the natural instinct for connecting with a small child.

She forced her thoughts back to the present as they mixed the batter and formed it into balls. "Now for the best part. We get to roll them in cookie crumbs." She opened the box of vanilla wafers. "We need crumbs. Let's smash the cookies." She handed Sean a mallet and he pounded vigorously. "Now let's roll the cookies in the crumbs."

Again everyone helped. Sean ate one cookie, and the rest were set aside for dessert.

Sean and Kelly washed the dishes and put them away. As she watched them talk and work, Nancy said, "I haven't had this much fun in years."

Kelly smiled. She was certain Sean would profit from spending time with the Hamiltons. They were good for him, perhaps better than his father, she admitted to herself with a sigh.

Later, when Sean went upstairs for a nap, she sat in the living room with Joe and Nancy.

"We'll be back again Thursday," Nancy said.

"Lynn Eldridge and I made a date to take the kids to the Blue Bell Creamery in Brenham to see the ice cream being made," Kelly said. "Could you come Friday?"

Nancy shook her head. "We have plans. We'll have to make it Thursday. I'm sure you and Mrs. Eldridge could take the children next week."

Though Nancy's tone was pleasant, she left no room for argument, and Kelly remembered the day Nancy had insisted she meet her in the park. "All right," she agreed.

Apparently satisfied with Kelly's capitulation, Nancy asked, "Are all your students Sean's age?"

"Only a few. Preschoolers are my favorites though. I'd like to work with them full time. In fact, I plan to."

"You're not thinking of leaving Cedar Grove?"

"Not yet. But someday I intend to start my own preschool for children with language problems." Kelly found herself sharing her dreams with Joe and Nancy, describing in detail the school she'd pictured for so long.

"When you're ready to start, we'd like to help out," Joe said. "Perhaps give a gift for furniture or materials."

"Thank you. I'll keep that in mind and let you know," Kelly promised. She'd contact them when her plans were under way, she decided when they left, even though she knew people often made spur-of-the-moment promises that never materialized. Still, Joe had been kind to mention it.

She told Grant about Joe's offer when she spoke to him that evening and was surprised at his reaction. "Oh," he mumbled. Clearly, he didn't want to talk about the Hamiltons. He didn't even enjoy hearing about their part in Sean's activities.

That weekend, when she told him they'd visited again, his jaw clenched and he became his old silent self.

He did, however, take Sean fishing on Saturday afternoon. He might not care for his late wife's parents, but Kelly was gratified to see that he was learning to enjoy his son and their time together.

The following week was a repeat of those before it, with one exception. Grant called every evening. They talked about Sean's progress, but Kelly omitted any mention of the Hamiltons. They discussed Grant's work, and she sensed that telling her about his days was good for him. And they chatted about anything else that came to mind—their childhoods, their mutual love of horses, Grant's interest in architecture, his long-ago trip across Europe, visiting castles and cathedrals. Every evening, Grant concluded their conversation with the same words: "I think of you," and Kelly would respond in kind.

She thought of him too much. She thought of the man she was coming to know. A passionate lover, a dedicated businessman, a man of many interests. Though she'd learned more about him, she still saw the barrier, high and impenetrable, that he placed between himself and the world. Even during their most intimate moments, Kelly couldn't scale it.

She wondered how their affair would end. Despite his assurance that he wouldn't hurt her, Kelly had a premonition the end would be painful. She doubted Grant was ready for a permanent relationship. The portrait of Claudia stayed in her mind. How much more must the real woman dominate Grant's memories?

When the phone rang on Thursday evening, Grant's voice conveyed tension, temper. "What's wrong?" Kelly asked.

"How can you tell?"

It wasn't difficult. Love had sensitized her to every nuance of his speech. "You sound upset."

She heard his sigh. "Nancy called this morning. She and Joe want Sean to spend the first week of July with them."

"Don't you want him to go?"

"No."

"What did you tell them?"

He sighed again. "I told them yes after Nancy pointed out their time in Texas is limited and they want to spend as much as they can with Sean. She's very demanding."

Kelly had to agree. Nancy did seem to be a woman who expected to get what she wanted. Yet, her argument for having Sean spend a week with her and Joe appeared reasonable.

Kelly and Grant had talked last weekend about taking Sean to the Fourth of July activities in La Grange. She wondered if Grant was upset because he didn't want to miss the time with Sean or because he disliked the Hamiltons.

"Joe and Nancy will come out Saturday afternoon to pick him up," Grant continued.

Since Sean would be gone, Grant probably wouldn't come home, Kelly thought with sudden disappointment, but he said, "I'll see you Friday night."

"You're . . . you're still coming?"

"Yes. I need to see you. Now more than ever."

NINE

When Grant arrived Friday evening, Kelly could feel his tension. Although he joined her and Sean in a game of Old Maid after dinner and read Sean his bedtime story later, he seemed preoccupied. When he finished the story, he lifted Sean into his arms and held him close. Kelly saw pain in Grant's eyes, the same raw anguish she'd observed after their first meeting when Pat Ferris had spoken to him about Claudia.

Was his dead wife again on his mind? He'd been upset about her parents' coming for Sean. Perhaps seeing them would bring back too many painful memories.

Kelly left Grant and Sean and wandered down the hall to her room, where she sat on the bed and stared out the window at a cloudy evening sky. She should go downstairs, watch television, or read; but she, too, was fixated on Claudia, wondering if Grant could ever let go of her memory.

At last she heard his knock at her door. For a moment, she was tempted to tell him to go away, but he knocked again, and as though she were a marionette tugged by a string, she walked to the door and opened it.

119

Grant stood in the hall, his face haggard, his eyes dark and troubled. His pain, whatever its origin—Claudia or not, became hers. She drew him inside and put her arms around him. "What is it?" she asked. "What's wrong?"

He buried his face in her hair. "I need you," he whispered.

She couldn't say no. No matter how he felt about her, about Claudia, she loved him. She drew back and nodded. He took her wrist, his grip almost too hard, and led her to his room. Kelly could hardly keep up with his hurried strides.

Inside, he shoved the door closed and pulled her into his arms. He kissed her deeply, roughly, then jerked the blouse from her waistband and unbuttoned it with fumbling haste.

She reached for the buttons of his shirt, but with an impatient murmur, he pushed her hands away and undid them himself, then pulled her against him. He groaned as her naked breasts met his chest. He held her so tightly she could hardly breathe; his heart pounded against hers; his breath came fast and harsh. Wanting to soothe, she put her hand to his cheek, but he shook his head and tightened his hold until she gasped. He seemed not to notice. She hadn't expected this from the man who'd been so gentle with her before. Not this fierce demand, this obliviousness to her own needs.

"Your jeans," he muttered. Before she could move to help him or refuse, he had them undone and down her legs. In seconds he had yanked off the rest of his clothing.

Hands on her waist, he lifted her as if she were weightless. Powerless to resist him even now, she wrapped her legs around him; he carried her to the bed and followed her down.

He drove into her, thrusting again and again, harder and deeper. This wasn't love; it was anger, despair, an agony so profound that Kelly could only hold him until it ran its course.

With a desperate cry, he plunged one last time, then collapsed on top of her. Kelly bore his weight, stroked his sweat-soaked back and damp hair until his shudders died away and his breathing calmed.

He shifted and lay on his back, his arm covering his eyes. "I'm sorry," he said in a broken whisper. "Did I hurt you?"

"No." Not physically, but she felt torn, drained. For a moment, she wanted to run from the force of his emotions, but love, compassion made her stay. "Something's tearing you up inside," Kelly said. "Talking might help."

"There are certain things I can't talk about," he said so low she could barely hear.

She touched his cheek "Try. I want to understand."

"I've lived with this a long time," he began, his hand still shielding his eyes, "but the idea of Sean's spending a week with the Hamiltons brought all those feelings to the surface."

That was an understatement, Kelly thought. Whatever was bothering Grant had spewed forth like a volcano. "I can see you don't care for them."

"I don't care to have Sean spend time with them."

Though she was taking a risk by asking, she couldn't help saying, "Don't you want Sean to know his mother's family?"

"No." His answer was sharp, final.

"But why?"

"Because of Claudia."

This was the first time he'd mentioned his wife by name. *Claudia.* Just hearing it made Kelly numb, sick. Yet she forced herself to listen.

"I fell in love with Claudia the moment I met her. She was beautiful, perfect—like a goddess."

A goddess, Kelly thought. Yes, she'd felt that, too, just from seeing Claudia's portrait.

Grant sat up, elbow on his knee, and stared at a spot on the wall as if he could see Claudia before him. "I thought I had the world by the tail. Gorgeous wife, growing business.

"The first year we were married was heaven. We bought a little house, spent every evening and weekend together. I was wrapped up in her; I thought she felt the same way." He gave a sudden harsh laugh. "Then we joined the country club, bought a big house. That was the turning point. Our marriage began to sour. It became a nightmare that grew worse year by year."

Kelly stared at him in shock. Nightmare? Worse? She'd expected just the opposite—avowals of undying love, expressions of heartbreak. "I . . . I don't understand."

"Claudia got involved with the society crowd and became obsessed with keeping up with them. For a while, I thought she was going through a phase, and I'd joke about her jet set friends, but Claudia was dead serious. She was spoiled . . . always had everything she wanted from her parents and expected the same from me." He spoke in sharp, staccato bursts. "She wasn't satisfied . . . with me . . . with what I gave her. God knows, I tried."

"What did she want?"

"Money . . . excitement . . . prestige."

"She was a fool," Kelly murmured, sitting up and touching Grant's arm. Claudia had Grant. What more could she have needed?

"I worked hard. I built up my business," he continued, "but the money I made was never enough for her."

Kelly tried to digest this information. She remembered a comment Lynn Eldridge had made about Claudia. "She was always looking for glamour and excitement." And she recalled Lynn's attitude, her voice when she'd discussed Grant's late wife. She hadn't liked the woman. Now Kelly understood.

"I tried, I really tried to please her," Grant went on. "I wonder sometimes if I could have done more."

Kelly could see guilt gnawing at him. She put her hand on his. "I'm sure you did everything you could."

He turned his hand and grasped her fingers. "What I did was work longer hours. While I worked, Claudia partied. We hardly saw one another, just kept drifting farther apart."

Now that he'd begun talking, the words spurted out as if they'd been dammed up for years and were now set free. "We argued, but Claudia was good at getting her way, and things didn't change. I made money; she spent it. My life was the office, hers was the latest society bash. I decided I couldn't take any more. I told her I wanted a divorce." He paused and Kelly held her breath. "She told me she was pregnant."

"Sean," Kelly murmured.

"Yes. Everything changed for me then. I was ecstatic."

"You wanted this baby?"

"More than anything."

Again, an unexpected statement. From all she'd seen of Grant in those first months—from their initial conference to their trip to the zoo—she'd have bet a baby was the last thing he'd wanted. "B . . . but—"

"But what happened to change my attitude?"

She nodded.

"For a while, our relationship improved. In fact, it was almost a repeat of the early days of our marriage. Waiting for the baby, watching Claudia grow big with my child was an incredible experience for me. But I soon found out that, while my outlook changed, Claudia's was the same. She partied as much as ever, maybe more."

"What happened?"

"We started arguing again. Mostly about her social life. I wanted her to take better care of herself, stop smoking, slow down. She said she wanted to enjoy herself before she was tied down with a baby. That was a joke," he said bitterly. "Nothing would have tied Claudia down."

"Didn't she want to be careful, for the baby's sake?" The idea of a mother-to-be unconcerned about her baby's welfare was incomprehensible to Kelly.

"I don't believe Claudia ever gave a thought to the child," Grant said. "He was just a temporary inconvenience, taking up space in her body. She worried more about missing a party when her ankles swelled or about stretch marks than about the baby."

Kelly didn't answer Grant's bitter tirade. What could she say?

"A week before Sean was due we had the fight to end all fights. Not a physical fight, of course—a battle of words. I came home early for a change and found her getting dressed for a night at the club. I told her we needed some time together. She said she didn't need that kind of time. I shouted at her that we were having a baby, for God's sake, and if we were going to build a family, we needed to start building a relationship."

He stopped to draw a ragged breath. Again, Kelly waited.

"She began to laugh. I asked her what the hell was so funny, and she said, 'You. You think you can dictate a relationship. You think you can order me around over this baby.' 'You're damn right,' I told her. 'It's my baby.' 'Maybe it is,' she said. 'Maybe it isn't. You'll never know.' "

"My God," Kelly whispered. "You must have been devastated."

"Yes, I was destroyed." After a moment, he continued. "Claudia had a difficult labor and her doctor decided on a C-section. I sat in the waiting room thinking I should feel something, but I couldn't. I felt . . . nothing. When the baby was born, I could hardly look at him for fear of what I'd see. Someone else's face, someone else's genes."

"Grant." Kelly wanted to gather him into her arms, but she sat frozen, afraid he'd push her away.

"Two weeks later Claudia had a party to go to. I told her to skip it. She shouldn't have been driving yet, but she said two weeks without a social life was all she could stand. She got dressed and took off. The police called at three A.M. She'd run into a concrete abutment on the freeway. She died instantly."

Grant gave a harsh sigh, let go of Kelly's hand, and turned away. The room was still, with no sound except the faint hum of the air conditioner. Her eyes on Grant's slumped shoulders, Kelly prayed that she would do the right thing, say the right thing to bring solace to this tortured man.

At last he spoke. "Afterward, I couldn't relate to Sean. I tried at first, but every time I looked at him, I'd hear Claudia laughing, remember her words. Finally, I gave up trying. Olivia was here. I turned Sean over to her and shut him out of my life."

Kelly put her hand on his shoulder and felt him stiffen. "How can you touch me after hearing this?" he muttered.

"Oh, Grant," she whispered, drawing him into her arms. "You were hurting. You're still hurting. You need someone to hold you." She lay back, pulling him down with her and guiding his head to her breast.

After a long silence, she heard his breath escape in a ragged sigh. "I've never talked about this before."

"You've kept all that anger and pain bottled up inside." She stroked the rough stubble on his cheek. "No wonder you didn't have room for Sean." No wonder he'd wanted to avoid confronting Sean's problems. He must have borne an incredible amount of guilt. "And I ramrodded my way into your life, battering at all your defenses."

"No . . . no! You're the best thing that ever happened to Sean and to me. You wouldn't let me hide from him . . . from myself." He said earnestly. "Can you see now why I don't want Joe and Nancy around? Why I'm afraid to have Sean spend too much time with them? I'm so damn scared they'll turn him into a carbon copy of Claudia—spoiled, selfish. I couldn't stand it.''

Kelly chose her words carefully. ''Parents aren't always the cause of their children's behavior. Claudia might have acted the way she did because she was just . . . Claudia.''

''Maybe, but I don't want to take a chance with Sean. I don't have a choice though. If I say no, I'll antagonize Nancy and Joe. Besides, they'll be here only a few weeks.''

Kelly was glad he wasn't going to deny the Hamiltons their time with Sean. She didn't believe they would damage the child.

But now her concern was for Grant. As he lay rigidly beside her, she tightened her arms around him. She wanted to keep him close, keep him safe, soothe away his anguish. She began to stroke him gently.

''Kelly . . . you don't have to—''

''Shh, I want to.'' She stroked his shoulders and back, kneading the taut muscles, easing away the pain. He lay still, his ragged breaths slackening, his heartbeat slowing until she thought he was asleep.

Then she felt his lips against her shoulder, heard him whisper her name, and felt a different kind of tension in his body. She brushed her hand across his thigh; his arousal swelled against her, yet he made no move toward her. Was he ashamed because of what happened before? He needn't be. He'd been in the throes of an emotion so fierce he'd handled it the only way he could. She had to erase the memory of that angry coupling from his mind . . . and from hers.

She gathered him closer, opened for him, and guided him where he needed to be, where she needed him. Deep inside her.

Kelly set their pace, moving slowly at first, then

faster, harder, until Grant's breath caught, he cried out her name, and she felt his release and her own.

"Kelly," he whispered afterward. "Kelly, I'm—"

"Hush. Don't say anything. Just rest." She drew his head to her shoulder. "I'm going to hold you."

He sighed and relaxed again. Soon she heard the deep, even breathing that told her he was asleep. But Kelly lay awake, thinking, wondering.

Was Grant's perception of Claudia accurate, or was it colored by his own anguish? Then she remembered the pain in his voice as he'd repeated Claudia's words. "Maybe he's yours; maybe he isn't. You'll never know."

She thought of the portrait of Claudia—the beauty that belied the cruelty inside. How could she have planted that ugly seed of doubt in Grant's mind? That uncertainly that had turned him away from his only child?

If Claudia had wanted to make Grant suffer, she couldn't have chosen more effective means, but she'd injured Sean, too, with her viciousness. Surely, no mother would willfully hurt her child. Or would she?

And why had Grant believed her?

Kelly studied the man who slept in her arms. Repose had smoothed away the lines she'd seen in his face when he'd spoken of Claudia. He looked young, defenseless. A surge of protectiveness swelled in Kelly's heart. She'd always pictured Grant as he appeared on the surface—strong, assured, with a thick armor against the slings and arrows of life. That armor wasn't as thick as she'd believed. Or perhaps a woman with Claudia's wiles had known how to pierce it.

Another man might have reacted differently, disregarded Claudia's taunts, and given Sean the love his mother had rejected. But whatever insecurities lay beneath Grant's veneer of indifference hadn't allowed him to do that. Another man might have—

Kelly broke off her thought. She wasn't in love with

"another man." She cared for the man sleeping beside her, cared for him with an intensity she couldn't deny. She gathered him closer. Tonight she wouldn't leave him.

Grant's eyes opened to pale predawn light. He lay with his head pillowed on Kelly's breast, her arms wrapped around him.

He turned toward her, and her eyes flew open. "Grant?" She touched his cheek. "Are you okay?"

He nodded, then looked outside, as the first rays of sunlight erased the darkness. "You stayed all night."

"Yes."

She didn't offer a reason, but he knew why. She'd stayed because he needed her.

Now she sat up. "I'd better go. Sean'll be up soon." She hesitated a moment, then said, "You know, there are tests that could prove whether or not you're Sean's father."

"I know. I thought once about having one, but I wasn't ready. Now I don't need to."

Her brows furrowed. "I don't understand."

"I don't care anymore whether I'm Sean's natural father or not. He's my son. I know that now."

"Oh, Grant." She took his face in her hands and kissed him deeply. "I'm so glad, so very glad."

"So am I."

He watched her slip from the bed and gather her clothes. Her hair was tangled, and beneath her eyes, purple smudges gave evidence of a sleepless night; yet when she turned to him, her expression was solicitous. "Sure you're all right?" When he nodded, she bent over him and kissed him. "Go back to sleep for a while. I'll try to keep Sean quiet."

He caught her hand. "Thank you."

She shook her head. "You don't need to thank me."

But he did, he thought as he watched her leave. She'd listened to a story he'd never shared with anyone because he'd been too hurt and ashamed. She'd heard him out without disdain, without censure. And then cradled him inside her, held him in the shelter of her arms through the night, waited until he wakened, her concern only for him. He had no way to thank her, no words to tell her what her presence meant to him.

Had he at last found someone he could trust? Someone he could count on? Once he'd thought he could trust Claudia. That hadn't lasted long, but Kelly was different—warm, giving.

He turned and watched the sky lighten, saw the sun's rays gild a bank of clouds. Had life handed him another chance?

"Yes," he wanted to shout, but his natural wariness interfered. "Slow down," he reminded himself.

He'd been impulsive with Claudia, letting her beauty lure him into a relationship before he really knew her. He wouldn't make that mistake again. He'd listen to his mind this time as well as his heart. But he hoped his heart would win in the end.

The Hamiltons arrived after lunch. Grant greeted them stiffly and invited them to wait in the living room while Olivia got Sean ready to leave.

Kelly noticed that Joe and Nancy were equally cool. "I suppose you've been busy this summer," Joe remarked.

"Very."

Joe glanced at Nancy. "Too bad you can't spend more time with Sean."

Grant's lips thinned. "I see him on weekends."

"Children grow up fast," Nancy said. "He'll be ready for school before you know it. He'll be playing Little League and going to Cub Scouts. Then he won't have time for you."

Grant said nothing.

Silence grew in the room, and Kelly tried to think of something to say to ease the strain. Then Sean burst in. "Grandma, Grandpa. I'm going your house." He gave Joe a high-five, then scrambled into Nancy's lap for a hug.

Joe rose. "Well, young man, got everything you need?"

"I got 'jamas, got my bear, got Turtles."

"How about your toothbrush?" Nancy asked.

"Uh-huh. Got a toothbrush."

"Then let's hit the road," Joe said.

He and Grant shook hands without enthusiasm, Joe picked up Sean's duffel bag, and Nancy took the child's hand. "Good-bye, Grant. Kelly, we'll see you next weekend," she said.

Grant walked them to the door. When it had shut behind them, he let out a long sigh. Kelly released a breath, too, glad the almost-palpable tension was gone.

Grant held his hand out to her. "Let's go for a swim."

"All right. What time do you have to leave?"

"I don't."

A rush of anticipation surged through her as Grant pulled her close. "I'm glad. We have till tomorrow morning, then?"

"Huh-uh. We have all week."

"But how—?"

He laughed and bent to kiss the tip of her nose. "We have a holiday coming up, remember? I told Olivia she could take the week off. If you don't have any other plans, I thought we'd spend the time together, just the two of us."

Other plans? If she'd planned to get together with the president, she'd have canceled it. "I'm at your disposal, Mr. Stuart."

He touched his lips to hers. "Good. Let's make every minute count."

TEN

They spent a lazy hour by the pool, soaking up sunshine, sipping iced tea. "Let's drive to Houston for dinner tonight," Grant suggested.

Kelly hesitated. Taking Sean to dinner together at the local Dairy Queen was an acceptable part of her job, but dinner alone in a Houston restaurant—

He trailed a finger over her shoulder. "We'll go someplace quiet and romantic."

Why not? Why not throw caution to the winds and enjoy herself for one evening? The chances of running into someone they knew in a city the size of Houston were slim. "Quiet and romantic sounds nice," she said. Any place would be romantic with Grant, even a hamburger joint or a pizzeria.

He didn't choose either. He picked the Houston branch of Brennan's, the famous New Orleans restaurant. It mirrored the gracious charm of the French Quarter. Gaslights, oiled cypress woodwork, brown toile wallpaper bespoke the elegance of the old South.

Kelly wished she had a dressier outfit for the evening, but she hadn't thought she'd need one when she'd packed for the ranch. Her summer wardrobe consisted of shorts, jeans, and shirtwaists. For tonight she'd chosen a white silk belted with a wide turquoise sash and added Navajo jewelry.

When they'd reached Houston, she'd suggested stopping off at her condo so she could change, but Grant shook his head. "Why? You look fine . . . perfect." Flattered, Kelly had decided she didn't need different clothes after all.

At the restaurant, they sat on the patio amid palm trees and magnolias and sipped Sazerac while twilight faded into evening. Then the maître d' led them to a secluded table in the white-trellised garden room. They dined on rich turtle soup laced with sherry, watercress salad, and snapper Pontchartrain.

Kelly barely noticed the elegant ambience, the discreetly attentive service, or even the food. She had eyes only for Grant. Dressed in a smoke gray suit the color of his eyes, he projected an aura of assurance and ease in his surroundings. Gone was the tortured man of the night before . . . or was he hiding?

They ordered bananas Foster for dessert and watched the waiter prepare the flaming delicacy. When he had spooned it into their plates with a flourish, Kelly tasted, shut her eyes, and let the flavor of cognac, the sugary warmth of the bananas, and the chill of ice cream roll over her tongue. She ate slowly, savoring every sinfully delicious bite.

"Heavenly," she murmured, licking a tad of ice cream from her lip.

Grant's eyes fastened on her tongue. "Yes." His voice husky, he leaned toward her and touched a fingertip to her mouth. "You missed a spot. If we were home, I'd lick it off."

At his words a warmth, hotter than the brandy, ignited inside her. His finger lingered, feathering over her lips, parting them, and darting inside. Then, as if mindful of their surroundings, he returned his hand to the tabletop.

His eyes locked with hers. "I want to take you to

bed,'' he whispered, ''undress you in the lamplight. First the earrings.'' His hand wandered to her lobe and set the turquoise drop swaying, then slipped away again. ''I want to kiss you there,'' he breathed, sending a shiver of anticipation through her body.

His gaze trailed down her neck and along her collar. ''Silk,'' he murmured, ''but your skin is smoother. I want to unbutton your dress . . . slowly . . . slide it off your shoulders. I want to look at you in those lacy underthings . . . kiss you through them—''

She imagined his kiss heating her skin, tightening her nipples through the filmy silk. The image was so vivid, she felt her breasts swell, ache for his touch.

''—but not for long,'' he went on, making love to her with his words. ''I want to take them off. I want to see you . . . touch you . . . put my hands over your heart, feel it pounding . . .''

It pounded now, a wild cadence in her chest. Blood pulsed through her body, flushing her cheeks. Her breathing became shallow.

''. . . then carry you to bed and make love to you all night . . .''

''Grant,'' she whispered. ''I—''

''Coffee?''

Startled, Kelly turned and blinked at the waiter, who stood beside their table.

Grant shook his head. ''Check,'' he said hoarsely.

''I'll be right back, sir.''

As reality intruded, Kelly flushed with embarrassment, hoping the waiter hadn't overheard their graphic conversation. When he returned, Grant tossed a handful of bills on the table, rose, and pushed his chair back. ''Let's go.''

They hurried from the restaurant and waited impatiently for their car. *An hour's drive back to the ranch*, Kelly thought. *Too long. Much too long.*

She'd spent her adult life focusing on verbal communication, but she'd never thought of verbal *lovemaking* or imagined it could be as erotic as the act itself. But, for those moments in the restaurant, her body had burned with a flame every bit as bright as if she and Grant were in his bed.

What would the other patrons have thought if they'd guessed the man and woman sitting sedately at the corner table weren't discussing current affairs but engaging in a love affair? That they weren't talking about the summer heat but creating an inferno of their own? And she still burned.

When their car arrived, Grant shoved a bill into the valet's palm. As he sped away, he took Kelly's hand and laid it against his thigh. She felt his muscles quiver beneath her fingers.

Hurry, Kelly thought, but he exited the freeway after a few blocks. "Where are we going?" she asked, disappointed that his ardor had cooled so quickly.

"Honey, if you think I can wait an hour to have you, you have more faith in my control than I do. The way I feel tonight, La Grange is as far as the moon. We're going home."

In minutes, they pulled into the driveway of Grant's house. They rivaled one another in their rush to get out of the car. Two doors opened, slammed. Grant caught her arm, and they ran across the porch, both laughing with crazy exhilaration.

Grant shoved the door open and pulled her into his arms. His kiss was fiery, demanding, insatiable. Finally he tore his mouth away and swung her up against his chest. As he carried her up the stairs, Kelly clung to him dizzily. *Scarlett O'Hara, eat your heart out*.

In Grant's bedroom, they didn't bother with preliminaries. Why should they? Kelly thought; the entire evening had been foreplay. Their joining was as hot and swift as a shooting star. Afterward, she lay replete in Grant's embrace. He pulled the sheet over them and Kelly fell asleep.

In the morning she gradually became aware of a

heaviness on her chest. Eyes still shut, she mumbled, "Go 'way, Walter," and burrowed deeper beneath the cover.

"So," a masculine voice intruded, "she spends the night with me and wakes up thinking about Walter."

Kelly's eyes flew open. "Grant! I was sleeping so hard I forgot where I was."

"Apologies, apologies. A man feels pretty low when he can't compete with a cat."

Kelly rolled to her side and rubbed against him as if she were a cat herself. "Maybe if you try again . . ."

"A second chance, hm? I guess I should make the most of it." He pulled her beneath him and did.

They returned to the ranch in the afternoon and spent the next two days and nights absorbed in one another. Kelly began imagining their relationship might last. They seemed so perfectly in sync, so right for one another. By summer's end, perhaps Grant would see her as a permanent part of his life and Sean's.

On Tuesday, she lingered at the breakfast table after Grant had gone upstairs to shower. She longed to do this every morning for the rest of her life—to wake beside Grant, to greet a new day together, even to argue over editorials in the newspaper as they'd done today.

The phone rang once as she cleared the table. A few minutes later Grant, freshly shaved, came into the room. "Lynn called," he said. "She and Sam are having some friends in from Houston for a barbecue on the Fourth and want us to come."

Kelly stood still, a cup in one hand, a plate in the other. *Friends from Houston*. "What did you tell her?"

"I said yes. Why? Don't you want to go?"

She loaded the dishwasher, letting the clatter of dishes excuse her from answering. No, she didn't want to go. Friends from Houston could mean parents from Cedar Grove. And without Sean along, her relationship with Grant would be obvious. Did she want that? Could she risk it?

Grant touched her shoulder. "Kelly? Is something wrong?"

She spun around and snapped, "I wish you'd asked me first." She saw his confusion and was sorry she'd been so abrupt, but he'd taken her by surprise.

"I thought you liked the Eldridges," he said.

"I do."

"Haven't you and Lynn been getting together?"

She bit her lip. "Yes, but with the children."

"How is this different?" His tone was reasonable, but his eyes flashed.

Needing some time, Kelly opened the cabinet under the sink, took out the detergent, and was about to fill the dispenser when Grant's hand closed over her wrist. "Leave it."

She drew a breath, put the box on the counter, and said, "Let's sit down and talk."

"Yeah, I think we need to."

Kelly followed Grant into the breakfast room and sat across from him. An examination of his scowling face told her she'd have a hard time explaining her feelings. She wished she hadn't cleared their cups from the table. The conversation would seem more "friendly" over coffee.

With a sigh, she began. "Grant, think of my situation here. You hired me as Sean's therapist. Now Sean isn't home. How will it look, you and me showing up alone?"

"Exactly as it is, that we have a personal relationship."

"But—"

"But you don't want that, do you? Don't you find it hypocritical that you're willing to sleep with me but not go out in public together?"

"That's not true," she cried. "We went out for dinner Sunday night."

"Alone."

"Yes." That *was* the difference. "Grant," Kelly implored, "try to understand. I'm here as a professional. I've stressed that to Lynn. Now she and her friends, some of them Cedar Grove parents, will see me as . . ."

"As?" he prompted.

As your mistress. No, that was an antiquated term. What was the current label? *Lover.* Sounded nice, but the connotation hadn't changed. She let out a breath. "As if I'm having an affair with my employer."

"I don't like the expression, but since you put it that way, we *are* 'having an affair.' " He folded his arms across his chest and glared at her.

Frustrated, she met his angry gaze and tried again. "I told you about my relationship with Nick—"

"And you put me in the same category as that bastard?"

She'd said this all wrong. "Of course not. You're not like Nick, but you *are* my employer. And my reputation is important to me. It's vital to the success of my school."

Grant shook his head. "Do you think in this day and time our being together would make a difference to anyone?"

"I don't know," Kelly admitted, "but I won't take a chance."

His lips twisted. "I'll call Lynn back." He stalked out of the room.

Kelly remained at the table, staring at her hands, which were now trembling. What should she do? Go to the party to assuage Grant's ego? Stay at home and guard her reputation? Either decision held a built-in disaster.

She went into the living room. Grant stood in the hallway beside the telephone. Unaware of her presence, he had discarded his shield of anger, and Kelly saw a hurt, dejected man. Her heart constricted.

How could she have forgotten Claudia so quickly? The wound Grant's wife had inflicted still festered. And Kelly had just dealt another blow to Grant's fragile ego. She'd been misled by his outward confidence and overlooked the vulnerability that lurked beneath the surface. But she still had her reputation to think of.

She took a step toward him. "Grant."

The mask dropped back into place. "Her line's busy."

"Grant, I—" The ring of the telephone cut her off.

Grant answered, listened for a moment, then said, "I'll get the next plane out." He hung up and called for a reservation.

When he set the phone down, Kelly said, "What's wrong?"

He started up the stairs. "Contract problems," he replied without turning.

She followed him. "But tomorrow's the Fourth—"

He halted so suddenly she almost ran into him. "Holidays don't mean anything in these negotiations. Millions of dollars are tied up in that shopping center. Jobs are on the line."

Kelly followed him to his room, where he began tossing clothes in a bag. Striving to keep her voice steady, she said, "And my school depends on much more than money—most of all, on the reputation of its director. I can't sacrifice that."

He slapped the lid down on the suitcase. "You've made that clear enough. Besides, it's a moot point now. I'll call Lynn from the airport."

Kelly didn't want to end the weekend this way. She caught his arm as he strode past her into the hall. "Grant, stop. Let's not part in anger."

Looking suddenly tired and despondent, he sighed, "I understand where you're coming from. I just don't like it." Then he turned away.

Kelly went halfway down the steps, watched the door shut behind him, and listened to the roar of the Mercedes' engine. He'd said he understood her feelings. Surely after he had time to calm down, he'd call and they could talk things through.

But he didn't call, and though she picked up the telephone half a dozen times, she didn't phone him either.

She managed to get through the next two lonely days by keeping busy—swimming, riding, driving into town for a movie—until the Hamiltons arrived with Sean. As soon as the child leaped out of the car and ran toward her, Kelly's spirits revived. "Hi there, hot shot," she said, hugging him. "Did you have a great time?"

"Great time," he echoed. "I saw colors up in the sky. And noises. Fire trucks up there."

"Fireworks?"

His small brow furrowed. "Not fireworks. Fire . . . cookies."

"Firecookies," Kelly muttered. "Oh, you saw fire*crackers*."

"Yeah," he agreed, as if she should have known all along.

Nancy's eyes sparkled with amusement as she came up beside them. "You're a translator, too," she whispered to Kelly.

"A big part of my job," Kelly agreed.

Aloud Nancy said, "Sean saw firecrackers and ate hot dogs and potato chips and ice cream—"

"—and drinked a beer," Sean announced.

"A root beer," Joe added hastily, and Kelly chuckled. Laughing felt good after the last few days.

They went inside with Tex trailing behind them, tail pumping furiously. "Sean," Nancy said, "find Daddy and give him a hug."

"Daddy's not here," Kelly explained before Sean could scurry off. "He went back to Boston."

Nancy raised a brow. "Didn't he know we were bringing Sean today?"

"Yes, but—"

"Now, Nancy," Joe said, "you know Grant's a busy man."

Nancy nodded. "Yes, of course." She glanced at Sean, who was absorbed with the dog. "Sean doesn't seem disappointed. He's used to having Daddy gone."

"We'd better be on our way," Joe said. "We'll be back soon."

Olivia returned later that afternoon, and with Sean's activities and the housekeeper's cheerful presence, Kelly felt more like herself. When the weekend went by without word from Grant, she tried not to let his absence disturb her. But it did, and she became increasingly irritated with his attitude.

Sunday night she went for a walk, then noticed she was following the path toward the weeping willow where Grant had kissed her with such sweet passion. She turned and headed in the opposite direction.

She was angry at him, not just for herself, but for Sean. Would he let *their* misunderstanding keep him away from his child? The more she thought about Grant's behavior, the more exasperated she became. She kicked a stone in front of her.

All right, if he wanted to walk around with a black cloud over his head, let him. "So he had a disastrous marriage," she grumbled to a crow perched on a nearby branch, "does that mean he has to let it control the rest of his life? That he can't pull himself together and go on?"

The crow cocked its head.

"You're no help," Kelly grumbled to the bird. She kicked at another stone and stubbed her toe. "Ow," she muttered, picked up the offending rock, and flung it aside. The crow flew away.

Tomorrow, Kelly decided, she'd call Mr. Stuart and give him a piece of her mind. Anger at her she could tolerate, but she would not allow him to neglect Sean.

She tried him Monday morning and again on Tuesday, but he was out, nor did he return her calls. By

Wednesday she was incensed, half ready to fly to Boston and drag him home. She had her hand on the receiver to try him again when the phone rang.

"Kelly."

Something was wrong. "Grant, what's happened?"

His laugh was harsh. "How do you know something's happened?"

"I can tell by your voice." His tone was worlds away from the anger and hurt she'd heard last week. This sounded more like . . . like panic. "What's the matter?"

She heard a deep sigh. "I don't have time to talk now; I'm on my way to the airport. I'll see you tonight."

"You're coming home?" Something serious must have happened for him to leave Boston in the middle of a workweek.

"Yes. Do me a favor, please. Call the Eldridges and tell Sam I'm on my way. And ask Olivia to save me something to eat. I'll be late getting home from Sam's." Before she could ask any more, Grant hung up.

Kelly called Sam. He said nothing about the reason for Grant's visit, but she hadn't expected him to. She relayed Grant's instructions to Olivia, then took Sean for a swim. In the afternoon, they went on a bug hunt, then read *The Hungry Caterpillar* and glued a caterpillar body together from pieces of construction paper. The lesson was successful, but Kelly didn't enjoy it as she usually did. Tension crawled up her spine and tightened her muscles.

She heard Grant's car pull up around eleven and ran down the stairs to meet him. He started in surprise when he saw her. "Kelly?" he said, his tone wary. He looked rumpled and tired.

She forgot last week's argument. Nothing mattered but the weary sound of his voice, the defeated slump of his shoulders, and the need in his eyes.

She went to him and put her arms around him. He buried his face in her hair and held on. After a moment, he said, "You didn't have to wait up for me."

"I wanted to. Sit down in the breakfast room. I'll heat the dinner Olivia left out."

"No, just some coffee, please. I'm not hungry."

"Coffee will keep you awake."

"I'll be awake anyway," he said as he followed her into the breakfast room.

Kelly poured coffee and sat beside him. "What's wrong?"

He took a sip, then slammed the cup down. Liquid sloshed onto the table. He swiped at it distractedly, then looked up at Kelly. "This morning I heard from the Hamiltons, or rather from their lawyer. They're suing me."

"Suing you? But what for?"

"They've filed a custody suit. Nancy and Joe want Sean."

ELEVEN

Dumbfounded, Kelly stared at Grant. "But . . . but why?"

"Because they love him, their lawyer says."

Of course, the Hamiltons loved Sean, but to take him away from his father? How could they? She covered Grant's hand with hers and squeezed as if she could transmit courage with her grasp. "They can't," she insisted, as much for herself as for Grant. "They don't have a case."

Grant ran his free hand through his hair. "I'm afraid they do. They're charging me with neglect, and Sam says they may very well prove it."

"No!" She grasped his other hand and tightened her fingers. "We won't let them."

He disengaged his hands. "This isn't your problem."

"I've just made it mine." When he started to protest, she barged ahead. "We'll talk to the judge. I'll tell him how much time you've been spending with Sean, how you—"

"No, you won't. This won't be a simple hearing in a judge's chambers. The Hamiltons are insisting on a jury trial."

"A jury trial! Why?"

"Sam thinks they expect a lot of public sympathy."

Suddenly the implications hit Kelly. Helping Grant would involve testifying in front of a whole courtroom of curious spectators. Testifying not only about Sean, but about her relationship with his father. Baring her soul, exposing her private life, and seeing her reputation and her dreams go up in smoke. Staring eyes, wagging tongues . . . could she face that, even for the man she'd come to love? The thought made her feel ill.

Grant sensed her shock . . . and her hesitation. "Don't worry. I won't ask you to appear, and Sam will do everything he can to keep you out of the courtroom. The Hamiltons' lawyer may want a deposition, but—"

"Stop!" She felt as if she were about to step off a cliff. This wasn't a choice she wanted to make, but did she *have* one? Could she balance her reputation against a father's love for his child? No, she had to testify because it was the right thing to do. She'd worry about the consequences later. Drawing a breath, she took the plunge. "If I have to appear, I will. In fact," she added, her conviction growing stronger, "I want to. I'm on your side."

"You don't realize what you're offering. I know you value your reputation. I won't let you risk it."

Frustrated, she slammed her hand on the table. "That decision isn't yours to make. It's mine."

A month ago she might have made a different choice, but that was before she'd seen how much Grant had suffered, how much Sean now meant to him. The reputation she'd worked so hard to cultivate might go, but that couldn't concern her now, not with the stakes so high. What was losing her reputation compared to the loss Grant would experience if Sean's grandparents took him away? Grant had just found his son. She wouldn't let him lose his only child.

Grant gripped her shoulders and gave them a shake.

"You're not making sense. We're talking public testimony."

"I know."

"Last week you wouldn't go to a barbecue with me, and now you want to appear in court on my behalf. Think about it."

Kelly leaned forward. "Last week was inconsequential, a party, for heaven's sake. This is your life we're talking about. Yours and Sean's. I won't let you lose Sean without a fight."

He stared at her, as if he couldn't believe what she'd said, as if he couldn't believe she was real. His hold on her shoulders eased. "You'd do this for me?"

When she nodded, he let out a long, ragged breath. "Come here," he whispered and pulled her onto his lap. He held her tight against him, kissed her deeply, desperately. She felt the emotions surging through him and tried to absorb them into herself.

At last he tore his mouth away and buried his face against her throat. "Ah, Kelly," he whispered. "You give me more than I have a right to expect."

"No." Words of love hovered on her lips, but she bit them back. This wasn't the time for Grant to hear her feelings; he'd had enough to absorb today. Instead, she touched his cheek. "Come upstairs."

He nodded, and hand in hand, they went up. In Grant's room, in his bed, Kelly gave him what she couldn't yet put into words . . . all the love, all the tenderness and care in her heart.

During the night Kelly went back to her room. Though she longed to stay with Grant, they still couldn't take a chance on Sean's finding them in bed together. Soon after sunrise, she heard Sean padding down the hall, then Grant's voice calling him.

"Daddy, when you got home?"

"Last night, son. Come give me a hug."

Kelly's heart wrenched. He'd called Sean "son," perhaps for the first time.

She listened to the sound of their voices, then their footsteps on the stairs. From her window she saw them heading for the stable, hand in hand. Two figures—a tall man, a curly-haired child—the love between them apparent in the clasp of their hands, the way Grant's head bent toward Sean's, even the way he adjusted his stride to the child's. How could the Hamiltons destroy what had been so newly won?

She asked the question again when Sam Eldridge and Grant met to go over their strategy for the trial, and Sam responded, "It's rotten, but this kind of thing happens more than you'd imagine."

The two men sat at the dining room table, Grant's pocket-sized tape recorder between them, a pile of papers scattered about, and a couple of empty coffee cups shoved to one side. Sam had asked Kelly to join them.

"We don't have much time," he said. "We're scheduled to go to trial in two weeks. Kelly, we need your input. The Hamiltons are sure to bring up Sean's language delay."

"Yes, when I met them, they remarked about the teacher noticing it instead of Grant. I told them parents who have no other kids to compare with may not be aware of a delay."

"Good argument. We'll also counter with the fact that, once the delay was mentioned, Grant immediately enrolled Sean in treatment. Now, what measures do we need to show how much progress Sean has made?"

"A language evaluation, of course."

"Can you do that?"

"I don't think I should," Kelly said. "Since I'm treating him, you'd have a stronger case if someone else evaluates him."

"Why?" Grant asked. "I trust you more than anyone else."

"No, she's right," Sam said. "They could shoot

her down for being biased. We need someone who's uninvolved and objective. Who do you suggest, Kelly?''

"Harriet Barber at Children's Hospital. Sean should have a psychological, too, to determine his intelligence and his emotional stability.''

"Right again,'' Sam said. "I already have that on my list. If we can prove Sean's a happy, well-adjusted kid, we bolster our case.'' Kelly gave him the names of two highly respected child psychologists, then Sam said, "Kelly, about your testimony—''

"Absolutely not!'' Grant said. "She's not going to testify.''

Kelly ignored Grant and spoke to Sam. "And I say I am.''

"Good,'' Sam said. "I planned to subpoena you anyway.''

"Sam—'' Grant began.

"Shut up, Grant. We need her testimony. Kelly, we'll talk about this in private.''

She nodded, then asked, "Sam, what are the chances?''

"Sixty-forty in our favor,'' he said with a grin so confident that Kelly smiled back. "I'm an old street fighter,'' Sam went on, "and I'm going to see those two get what they damn well deserve.'' Then, with a wicked grin, he added, "But I'm going to do it in style.''

Grant smiled, the first smile Kelly had seen since he arrived. "First class, right, Sam?''

"Yeah.'' He turned to Kelly. "You've spent time with the Hamiltons. What were your impressions?''

Kelly forced herself not to squirm and tried to answer as fairly as possible. "You may be disappointed, Sam. Joe and Nancy are wonderful with Sean, and I think they're decent people who want to do what's best for him.''

Grant's face darkened. "And that means taking him away from me?"

"They seem to think so," Kelly said. "I'm not saying they're right—" She realized that once she might have agreed with the Hamiltons, that only a few weeks ago she'd asked herself if Sean wouldn't be better off with his grandparents. "But they probably feel they can spend more time with him."

Grant snorted. "So could a lot of grandparents. My father's retired. That doesn't mean he'd steal my kid."

"Calm down, Grant," Sam warned.

"Don't tell me to calm down, dammit," Grant growled, face flushed and hands clenched. "Sean isn't a prize to win or a piece of property to go to the highest bidder. He's my son, he has a home here, with me. And that's where he's going to stay."

"Hey, easy," Sam said. When Grant continued to glower at him, he shrugged and said, "Okay, pal. You can yell and curse and pound the table as much as you want here, but when you get on the witness stand, you'd better not show your temper."

"Don't worry," Grant said. "I'm not moronic enough to throw a tantrum in the courtroom. Still, I'd like to run into Joe Hamilton in a dark alley one night. I'd wring his neck."

"Then I'd be defending you for assault and battery," Sam advised with a wry smile. He leaned back and stretched. "I think we need a break. I'll make some calls to set up the evaluations, and Grant can work off steam by running around the stable or pitching hay."

When Sam had gone into the other room, Grant said, "Let's take a walk. I want to talk to you." His expression was serious.

"Hey, I thought Sam told you to relax. Jog around the stable. Muck out the stalls."

"Huh-uh. No jogging, no mucking. There are more interesting things to do in a stable."

When her face turned beet red, Grant laughed and

kissed the tip of her nose. She'd lightened the mood for a moment at least. Taking his hand, she urged him outside.

Nothing moved, not a leaf or a blade of grass. Summer sunlight blazed down, casting the world into heat-induced lassitude, as silent as it was motionless. No birds called, no breeze stirred the trees. Even Tex, who usually barked incessantly, was too lazy to do anything but blink at them and go back to sleep.

"Kelly," Grant said finally, "I won't let you do this."

She took his face between her hands—the face she'd come to love. "You have no choice. You need me."

"Yes, I need you, but not to testify. You were right last week about the barbecue. I acted like an a—"

"Like a man who had his feelings hurt. We were both angry, but that's over."

Grant pulled her against him. "I don't deserve you," he whispered.

"But you have me." *Forever if you want.*

He drew away. "I'm going to tell the Hamiltons about Claudia."

"Grant, no!" Shocked, she grasped his shoulders. "You can't."

"If they realize the truth about Claudia could come out in court, they may withdraw their suit."

"Don't, Grant. Telling them may make them more determined to get Sean." Grant started back toward the house, and Kelly hurried to keep up with him. "Have you talked to Sam about this?"

"No, but I'm going to. Right now."

"He'll say no."

"Then I'll tell them after the trial."

"Do you think they'll believe you?"

He walked faster. "If they knew their daughter, they will."

"Grant!" She grabbed his arm and forced him to stop. "Don't. Please don't."

He scowled. "Why are you protecting them?"

"Out of compassion. I know you're angry, but think. Joe and Nancy lost their only child. Don't destroy the memories they have of her. Telling them about Claudia won't change things; it will just hurt them."

He stared at her for a moment, his gaze as gray and cold as steel, then said, "I'll talk to Sam."

Kelly left them in the dining room and went up to check on Sean. She found him still asleep, curled up with his teddy bear in one arm and his thumb in his mouth. She closed his door gently and went downstairs to get some iced tea.

When she passed the dining room, she heard Sam's raised voice through the closed door. "Stuart, are you out of your bloomin' mind? No way in hell will you tell the Hamiltons. Not your child? That'd be like handing the kid to them on a silver platter. Forget it, or get yourself another lawyer."

Kelly chuckled. Obviously, Sam shared her views.

She heard Sean calling and went back upstairs, determined to get the child out of the house for the afternoon. He was bound to feel the tension vibrating in the air. "Hey, hot shot. Let's cook dinner for Daddy tonight."

"O—*kay*."

"Shall we make hot dogs?" That was the extent of Sean's culinary prowess.

"Hot dogs," he agreed. "We can have pisghetti, too?"

"*Can* we have spaghetti, too?" Kelly said. "No, just hot dogs."

Sean stuck out his lip. "Pisghetti, too."

Kelly ruffled his hair. "Don't press your luck, buddy. You can have spaghetti *or* hot dogs, not both. Come on. Let's go to the store. What do we need?"

The change of subject caught his interest. "Hot dogs, mussard—"

"Yes, mustard."

"—and buns."

Still planning, they left the house. Their shopping trip was lengthened by several rides on the grocery store's mechanical horse, a stop for fish food for Sean's rapidly growing aquarium, and ice cream at the Dairy Queen.

Sam's car was gone when they returned, and Grant was nowhere to be seen. Kelly hoped he was relaxing. She herded Sean into the kitchen and together they prepared dinner—hot dogs, potato chips, and Sean's other specialty, butterscotch pudding.

"Mmm. Sean, this is delicious," Grant said later as he took a bite of mustard-slathered hot dog. The child glowed at his father's approval, and Kelly raised her glass of milk in salute to Grant, who valiantly took another bite. "Did you cook this all by yourself, son?"

"Kelly helped."

"A therapist, definitely. A chef, questionable," Grant said, raising his glass in return. Nevertheless, he cleaned his plate, then polished off the lumpy pudding.

After they'd put Sean to bed, Grant poured two glasses of wine, and they wandered out to the porch. Sitting close together on the wicker loveseat, they sipped wine and watched the stars.

Grant groaned and rotated his head from side to side. "I wish this mess was over."

"Two weeks. Then you'll have it all behind you."

"I hope."

"You will. Everything's going to work out." She set her glass down and began to knead his shoulders. "When the trial's finished, you should get away."

"Yeah, somewhere peaceful and relaxing." He moved to give her better access to his neck. "Ah, that feels wonderful."

She wanted to keep his mind off the trial, so she asked, "Where would you like to go?"

"Let's see," he murmured, shutting his eyes as she

continued her slow, calming movements. "Maybe an uninhabited island."

"In the South Seas?"

"Ummm. Or the Caribbean. Anywhere, as long as it's quiet."

"No people around," she agreed. "You can watch the sunrise and walk on the sand and swim—"

"We."

"Hmm?"

"Both of us," he said, turning back and slipping his arm around her shoulders. "You'll come, too."

"Okay." Laying her head on his shoulder, she gave in to the fantasy. "At night we'll build a fire on the beach and cook dinner."

"No hot dogs."

She chuckled. "Steaks. Or conch, fresh from the ocean."

"And after dinner we'll make love while the fire dies."

She pictured them on the sand, with the moonlight playing over their bodies and the pounding surf setting the rhythm for their lovemaking. She shut her eyes and enjoyed their dream.

During the next two stress-filled weeks, they returned to the dream again and again. Even though it was an illusion, it gave them something to cling to as the trial loomed nearer.

Kelly tossed an extra pair of hose in her overnight bag and zipped it closed. She wanted to leave for Houston early so she'd have time to go by Marla's and check on Walter before Grant got in. Although, as a potential witness, she couldn't go into the courtroom with him tomorrow, she intended to be at the courthouse to offer support. Even if she had to pace the floor outside the courtroom all day, Grant would know she was near.

Grant phoned as she was starting out the door. "You're not in Houston already, are you?" she asked.

"No," he said, sounding frustrated, "I'm still in Boston. We sat on the plane for an hour, then they told us to get off. They're unloading our baggage and putting us on another plane. God knows how long that'll take."

"Oh, no. Shall I call Sam for you?"

"Please. Tell him I'll check in when I get to Dallas."

"All right," she said. "I'll see you tonight."

But he didn't arrive. Instead, he called from Dallas. "I've missed the last plane to Houston. I'll be on the first flight out tomorrow morning. Since we're not scheduled to be in court until afternoon. I should be there in plenty of time."

But when Kelly reached the courthouse at one-thirty, Sam was alone, sitting outside the courtroom. "What's wrong? Where's Grant?" she whispered, conscious that the Hamiltons and their attorney, Aaron Lipscomb, were seated a few feet away.

"Somewhere between here and Dallas."

"What do you mean? He had a six A.M. flight. He should have been here hours ago."

"Haven't you listened to the news this morning?"

Kelly's stomach clenched as she shook her head. Had there been an accident, a plane crash? "Wh . . . what's happened?" she choked.

"Bad weather. Dallas has had severe electrical storms and major flooding. Both airports shut down."

She sagged into a chair. At least Grant wasn't lying unconscious in a Dallas hospital. Then she realized the ramifications. "Oh, no. He won't get here on time."

"It's beginning to look that way. He called and said he'd waited until seven, hoping the weather would clear. Then he decided to rent a car."

"That's over six hours ago. He should be here by now." Again, her imagination went to work. He'd driven his car into a flooded gully and drowned. He'd had a collision. He'd—

Sam's pager sounded, and Kelly jumped.

"My office," Sam said, checking the readout. "I hope it's a message from Grant."

Kelly started to get up, but Sam shook his head. "Stay here. The Hamiltons have been eyeing us for the past ten minutes. Let's not make them any more suspicious by racing to the phone." Kelly nodded and watched Sam stroll off.

She forced herself to sit still, though she wanted to pace. She kept her expression bland, though her jaws were clenched so tight they hurt. Grisly visions continued to play in her mind. *Stop*, she ordered herself, but couldn't obey. She stared at the elevators as if fixating on them could make Grant appear. Instead, a group of people emerged and walked single file after a uniformed deputy. The jury panel.

Finally Sam returned. "He's in Huntsville."

"But that's over an hour away."

"Right. He said the flooding was so bad it took two hours to get out of Dallas."

Kelly glanced again at the Hamiltons. Joe drummed his fingers on the arm of his chair; Nancy looked as cool and elegant as ever. "What are you going to do?"

"Go in and throw myself on Judge Ritter's mercy, then tell Lipscomb and the Hamiltons the truth. If the judge agrees, we'll get jury selection over this afternoon and begin testimony in the morning." He glanced down the hall at the Hamiltons, then muttered, "Oh, good God." His eyes fastened on the elevator, which had disgorged another crowd of people.

"What's wrong?" Kelly asked.

"See that fellow who got out of the elevator, the guy in the tan shirt? That's Dave Worley, court reporter for the Houston *Express*. Let's hope he's not covering our . . . oh, damn, looks like he is."

The man paused beside the Hamiltons, spoke to them, and pulled out a notebook.

"Great, just dandy," Sam muttered. "A custody suit to spice up the news. I'd better talk to Judge Ritter and get this show on the road."

Sam spoke to the bailiff, then followed him into the courtroom. His movements didn't go unnoticed. Lipscomb frowned after Sam, then motioned Joe to the side and said something to him while Nancy continued talking with the reporter.

Kelly's thoughts echoed Sam's. This was just what they didn't need—a reporter turning this trial into a three-ring circus. She picked up a magazine from the chair beside her and opened it, shielding herself behind it. Not that Dave Worley knew who she was . . . yet. But if he covered this story, he would, and so would everyone else in Houston.

Nancy, however, seemed delighted to have Worley's attention. She leaned forward, speaking animatedly, while Worley took notes.

At last Sam emerged from the courtroom and approached the Hamiltons' attorney. After listening, he beckoned to his clients, and the four of them stood in a little knot, talking earnestly while Dave Worley stared at them, his pencil poised. Finally Joe nodded, and Lipscomb and Sam went into the courtroom.

Nancy and Joe followed them as far as the door while the *Express* reporter ambled along behind them. Then Nancy turned to Joe and said, loudly enough for Kelly—and for Dave Worley—to hear, "Isn't that typical? Sean is always second to Grant's business affairs. He cares so little for that child he couldn't even get here on time for the trial."

Kelly's jaw tightened even more. No use pointing out to the Hamiltons that Grant was probably more frustrated and upset than they were about the day's events. Kelly was certain that they and their lawyer would slant their account of the delay so it suited their case and that Dave Worley, who was now scribbling furiously, would print Nancy's comment.

Though they might be sincere in their love for Sean, the Hamiltons were going to milk this trial for all it was worth.

TWELVE

"Mr. Lipscomb, you may call your first witness."

Judge Matthew Ritter's voice rang through the court-room, and the twelve jurors turned expectantly as Lipscomb responded, "Your Honor, the plaintiffs call Alyssa Drake."

Grant's muscles tightened into steel knots, but he drew a careful breath and wiped all traces of emotion from his face. He rested his hands on the polished oak table and stared at the front of the courtroom where the judge sat, flanked by the American and Texas flags. Then his gaze shifted to the witness stand as Alyssa Drake raised her hand and promised to tell the whole truth, so help her God.

Did she know the truth? Or only Claudia's version? Did she care? He doubted it, and even if she did, she was here for the Hamiltons, for Claudia, not for him. There'd been no love lost between Grant and Alyssa.

His eyes flicked over her, from her fashionably coiffed blond hair, past a face that graced society pages from Houston to Paris, down to hands folded modestly in front of her. Several of the jurors gaped at her champagne-colored silk suit. It probably cost more than many of them made in a month.

Grant wondered if Alyssa had told the *Express* reporter about the trial. She never missed a chance to get her name in the papers, and though she was a minor player in this scenario, she'd still see her name in print tomorrow. That would be good for her . . . and for the *Express*. This morning they'd given the trial a small article on an inside page. With the promise of a juicy glimpse into the lives of jet-setters like Alyssa Drake, the story could be front-page material tomorrow.

Grant grimaced at the thought. He'd read only the headline this morning—HOUSTON DEVELOPER FAILS TO APPEAR FOR CUSTODY HEARING—then he'd thrown the paper across the room.

Now Lipscomb led Alyssa through background information about herself, then asked, "Were you acquainted with the late Claudia Stuart, Mrs. Drake?"

"Very well." Alyssa's voice was smooth.

"Did you spend time together?"

"Yes, we did. A great deal."

"Would you describe how you spent that time?"

Alyssa smiled. "We belonged to the same country club; we jogged several times a week and worked out, went to the same nutritionist. Health was important to Claudia." Several of the younger jurors smiled.

Grant controlled the urge to sneer. Claudia had become interested in nutrition when the "in" crowd had espoused healthy diets. Nevertheless, she'd continued to smoke excessively, failing to see the irony in that.

Grant glanced at a yellow legal pad that Sam had divided into two columns, one labeled *Theirs*, the other *Ours*. He made a mark in the *Theirs* column. "A point for Claudia," he murmured.

"What the hell does her interest in nutrition have to do with anything?" Grant muttered under his breath.

"Believe me, *everything* has something to do with this case," Sam whispered. "By the time they finish, your late wife will look like a cross between Joan of Arc and Mother Theresa."

"So what?" Grant muttered. "We're concerned with the Hamiltons, not Claudia."

"Lipscomb will get to them later."

"What other activities were you involved in with Mrs. Stuart?" Lipscomb inquired.

"Charitable activities," Alyssa replied. "When I chaired the annual benefit for juvenile diabetes, Claudia was one of my most active and dependable workers. She was on the board of the American Cancer Society, and she worked tirelessly for the food bank."

"So you would describe your association as one of mutual interest in good causes?"

Alyssa gave him a dazzling smile. "Yes, exactly."

Interest in social climbing, Grant wrote on Sam's pad.

Lipscomb continued. "Were you acquainted with Mrs. Stuart's husband?"

"Yes, I was."

"And do you see him in this courtroom?"

"Yes, I do." She gestured toward Grant, and the jurors' eyes turned to him. Grant kept his face impassive.

"Now, Mrs. Drake, was *Mr.* Stuart involved in any of these charitable activities?"

"Well, of course, the bulk of the work on these affairs is done by women's committees, but husbands do attend the benefits."

"And did Mr. Stuart . . . attend the benefits?"

Alyssa cocked her head. "On occasion. I would say rarely."

"So Mr. Stuart was not involved in his wife's activities?"

"Objection," Sam said. "Plaintiff's attorney is asking for an inappropriately broad conclusion."

"Sustained."

"I'll reword the question. Did Mrs. Stuart attend many of these charitable functions singly or with friends rather than in the company of her husband?"

"Yes, Grant . . . Mr. Stuart didn't make time for Claudia—"

"Objection," Sam interrupted.

"Sustained," Judge Ritter ruled.

"Mrs. Drake," Lipscomb said, "Do you recall the night that Claudia Stuart died?"

"Yes, very well. A group of friends had a get-together just two weeks after Claudia had given birth. She arrived late at the party, looking tired and distraught—"

"Objection," Sam shouted.

"Sustained. The jury will disregard the witness's description," the judge said. "You may continue, Mrs. Drake."

"Well, Claudia came late. She was alone. She'd driven her own car. I remember expressing surprise that she was doing that so soon after a cesarean section, but she said Grant . . . Mr. Stuart had refused to drive her. My husband offered to drive her home, but she insisted on driving herself, even though we could see she was shaky. I . . . I told her good night, and . . . and that was the last time I saw her."

"Thank you, Mrs. Drake. That will be all," Lipscomb said and sat down with a self-satisfied smile.

The judge motioned to Sam. "Mr. Eldridge."

"Just a few questions, your honor," Sam said, rising. "Mrs. Drake, would you agree that these charitable activities you and Claudia Stuart engaged in also had a social aspect?"

Alyssa gave him a slow smile. "Of course. People are much more apt to donate to good causes when they're enjoying themselves, but the bottom line is raising money for charities."

"And the benefits themselves, are they expensive to attend?" Sam's voice was even, his manner one of simple curiosity.

"Yes," Alyssa agreed.

"Would you give us a rundown of the average cost

of participating in a benefit for . . . oh, say, juvenile diabetes?''

"Objection, your honor," Lipscomb said. "Irrelevant."

"On the contrary, it's quite relevant to my client's case," Sam countered.

"I'll allow the question," Judge Ritter said, turning to Alyssa. "You may proceed, Mrs. Drake."

She ran down the list of costs, and Grant saw several of the jurors gasp. If Sam meant to show them that Claudia had an expensive life-style, he'd succeeded.

"These affairs Mrs. Stuart attended without her husband," Sam continued, "did she ever attend with, say, another escort?"

"I, ah, don't recall," Alyssa said, but Grant heard the hesitation in her voice, and he hoped the jurors did, too.

"Thank you. That's all." Sam sat down and made a mark in the *Ours* column.

Throughout the morning an array of similar witnesses appeared. All were prominent in Houston society; all had names associated with charitable causes and civic improvement. All rhapsodized about Claudia's good qualities and indicated that Grant was notable by his absence from Claudia's side. And though Sam planted the idea in the jurors' minds that Claudia's activities were costly and that she didn't hesitate to enjoy herself in Grant's absence, the marks in the Hamiltons' column multiplied.

Grant felt his tension mount along with the tally. His jaw ached from clenching it; what had begun as a dull throbbing in his temples escalated to a full-blown migraine.

He tried to distract himself from the unflattering remarks of the witnesses by concentrating on the people around him. The judge needed a haircut. The court reporter had a run in her left stocking. One of the male jurors had an annoying habit of running his finger around the inside of his collar. One of the women had a mouthful of gum; her jaws worked incessantly.

None of these details diverted his attention from the testimony for long. He couldn't help but hear himself described over and over as an ogre. He wished Kelly were beside him.

At last the morning witnesses finished, and Judge Ritter called for a recess. Though Grant would have liked Kelly to join him and Sam for lunch, Sam insisted they not be seen together.

"Their stories sound like I was married to a saint," Grant said, shoving food around on his plate. "The Lady Bountiful."

"To be expected," Sam said.

"Well, it's damn unpleasant." Grant shoved his plate away.

"I won't deny that," Sam agreed.

"Besides, what does this have to do with Sean?"

Sam put his fork down. "Lipscomb's trying to portray you as a disinterested husband, ergo, a disinterested father." When Grant would have interrupted, he continued. "And you're playing right into his hands."

Shocked, Grant stared at Sam. "How? Dammit, I'm not doing anything."

"That's just the point. You're not reacting."

Grant reached for a roll, tore it in half, then tossed it on his plate. "I'm following orders." He heard a tremor in his voice and forced it to steady. "*You* told me to hold my temper."

"I didn't suggest you sit like a department store mannequin. You're wearing that arrogant, expressionless mask you put on so easily. *I* know you're hurting inside, but the jury sees you as a cold fish. Control your temper, but let your feelings show. Loosen your tie, muss up your hair, and let them see your pain."

Sam's words scared him. "I—"

Sam put his hands on Grant's arm. "I know you don't like to let anyone in on your private emotions, but make the effort. Your life and Sean's are on the line.''

Grant swallowed the lump in his throat. "Okay. I'll try.''

He gulped down two aspirin before they went back into the courtroom. The jurors filed in a few minutes later, and Grant studied them carefully. Sam was right, he realized. They weren't looking at him too kindly.

Although he didn't go so far as to take it off, he unbuttoned his jacket, and even that small alteration made him feel exposed. He wondered what those twelve people thought of him. Cold and unloving? An iceberg father? He realized, until recently, the description would have been deadly accurate. But he'd changed, and he had to make them believe it.

He loosened his tie. The movement made him feel foolish, but if Sam thought it would help the jurors see him as a regular guy, he'd do it. He'd show up in court in his underpants if it would help him keep Sean.

The afternoon began with testimony from friends of the Hamiltons. Like Claudia's cronies, the Hamiltons' friends stressed their good qualities. They'd been devoted to their daughter, they loved children, they were loyal, generous, warmhearted. Grant glanced at Nancy. *He* saw a selfish woman, determined to get her way no matter who suffered. A woman like Claudia. Didn't anyone else see through her facade?

Then testimony focused on Sean. First Principal Pat Ferris appeared and testified about his lack of language. On cross-examination though, Sam brought out Grant's immediate action once the school staff pointed out the problem.

Next, Marla Howard took the stand. "I imagine Cedar Grove has events involving parents," Lipscomb said to her.

"Yes.''

"Would you describe several for the jury?''

"We have an Easter egg hunt for preschoolers, a

spring festival in May with relays and other contests, and this year our class put on a play, *The Three Little Pigs*, for the parents.

"Did Mr. Stuart attend any of these events?"

"No. I believe he was out of town."

"So Sean Stuart was . . . unaccompanied by a parent?"

"Yes." She started to add something, but Lipscomb cut her off. "No further questions."

Sam rose. "Ms. Howard, was Sean Stuart the only child in your class whose parents didn't attend school functions?"

"No, there were several others. Children whose parents worked, particularly those whose work required travel."

"Mr. Lipscomb asked you if Sean was unaccompanied by his parent and you said he was. Was the child alone at these events?"

"No. The housekeeper, Olivia Stillwell, came with him."

"Thank you, Ms. Howard. You may step down."

The next witness was a child psychiatrist who had evaluated Sean and who described the consequences of lack of emotional closeness. "A child needs love and security during his early years so he can develop trust. The loss of Sean's mother made his need for closeness even more critical. Without that closeness, he could become frightened, lonely, insecure. He might retreat into a fantasy world to make up for deficiencies in the real world."

"Doctor, would you describe your examination of Sean Stuart?" Sam inquired during cross-examination.

"I met the child, talked with him, and observed his play," the psychiatrist replied.

"How long was your examination?"

"Objection," shouted Lipscomb.

"Overruled."

Sam repeated the question. "Thirty minutes," the doctor replied.

"And in that *brief* examination, did the child exhibit the behaviors your described—retreat into fantasy, insecurity, fear?"

"No, but the examination lasted only thirty minutes."

"Exactly," Sam said, nodding. Then he asked, "Doctor, you've testified to the importance of security during a child's early years, and you've made the point that such security comes from closeness with parents. Might a surrogate parent, someone who loved the child, spent time with him, provide the same closeness?"

"Yes."

"Then someone who spent time with Sean, someone like the housekeeper, might provide emotional security?"

"That's possible."

"Doctor, what would be the consequences of removing a young child from that source of security, placing him with different parent figures, in a different environment, perhaps even in a different country?"

The doctor hesitated, then clearly cornered, responded, "He might develop emotional problems."

"Thank you. You may step down." Sam made two marks in the *Ours* column.

Nancy Hamilton was the final witness of the day. Grant clenched his fingers as she walked to the stand. His headache, which had diminished in the past hour, returned full force.

React, Sam wrote on the pad and underlined it twice. Grant took a breath and let his emotions show—anxiety, emotional pain intensified by the migraine. He rubbed his head, clenched his hands, and even let his dislike of Nancy come through.

Lipscomb led Nancy through a description of the Hamiltons' visit to Houston in the spring. "When we came to the house, we found a silent, wary child. The housekeeper told us Sean had a language delay." Her voice broke. "He hardly spoke at all. Olivia explained he'd just been enrolled in a treatment program."

"Olivia Stillwell? The housekeeper?" Lipscomb asked.

"Yes."

"You got this information from the *housekeeper*?"

"Yes. Sean's father was out of town on business. The child was being raised by the housekeeper."

"Objection," Sam thundered.

"Sustained," said the judge. "Jurors, disregard the witness's last statement." But, of course, Grant thought, they'd already heard it.

"Mrs. Hamilton," Lipscomb continued, "have you seen your grandson since that first visit?"

"Yes, often. My husband and I are staying in Houston for the summer. We visit with Sean several times a week."

"Please describe those visits."

As Nancy's testimony proceeded, Grant didn't need Sam to remind him to react. He could hardly help it. Frustration, anger, and pain shot through him in turn. His cheeks flushed; his hands trembled, and in an effort to control them, he grasped a pencil. It snapped in half. The eyes of every juror fastened on the slivers of wood as Grant dropped them on the table.

"How many times would you estimate you've seen your grandchild?" Lipscomb asked.

"At least a dozen."

"And have you seen his father on any of those occasions?"

"Only one," Nancy said.

"Do you know where Mr. Stuart was on those occasions?"

"Out of town. In the past three months, as often as we've visited Sean, his father was home only once. Every other time, Grant was gone."

Grant shut his eyes as a fresh wave of pain and guilt

poured over him. He couldn't deny what Nancy said. If he lost Sean, and he very well might, he'd brought it on himself.

That night he lay in Kelly's arms and listened to the soothing sound of her voice. "Tomorrow will be better," she assured him. "You'll tell your side of the story, and the jury will see how much you love Sean."

"I hope."

"*I'll* make them see. When I testify—"

"Don't, Kelly."

"I have to. Sam says you need me." Her voice was firm. "I'll be in the courtroom tomorrow. And when this is over . . ."

Grant smiled. "We'll head for our island."

"We'll build sand castles on the beach . . ."

"Put on our snorkels and watch the fish . . ."

"Hunt for seashells . . ."

"And make love," Grant finished and pulled her closer for a preview.

Kelly waited outside the courtroom. She wouldn't be nervous, she assured herself, even though her appearance here would be splashed over the front page of the *Express*, even though she was certain every family from Cedar Grove was avidly following the trial. She wouldn't think of that or of this morning's headline on the front page of the City section: WITNESSES SAY DEVELOPER NEGLECTED WIFE AND CHILD. No, she'd go in, state her observations about Sean, answer questions, and leave. If only it were that easy.

"Ms. Connery." The bailiff motioned to her. Kelly squared her shoulders, took a calming breath, and followed him inside.

She avoided looking at Grant, though she felt his eyes on her. Instead, she surveyed the jury. Four men and eight women. Twelve strangers who would decide Sean's fate . . . and Grant's.

They were a cross section of ordinary Americans. Two grandmotherly-looking women, one of them in a soft blue blouse and skirt, the other in polyester stretch pants that clearly showed the bulges around her middle. A thirtyish woman dressed for success in a skirt and blazer and another woman of the same age dressed for comfort in city shorts and a sleeveless blouse. Were they mothers? Kelly hoped so. Mothers would understand the need of a motherless child for the stability only a father could provide.

The other jurors ranged from a bored young man with lanky blond hair who slouched in his chair, to an older gentleman who sat military-straight, to a grim-faced woman who stared at Kelly unblinkingly. *Please*, Kelly thought. *Please see through Grant's mask to the man underneath. See how much he loves Sean. How much he needs him.*

"Raise your right hand."

Kelly swore to tell the truth, then glanced once more at the jurors. They shifted in their seats, and the bulgy woman leaned forward, staring at Kelly as if she were the next chapter in a steamy novel.

Kelly turned her gaze to Sam, who gave her an encouraging smile. "Please state your name," he began.

He led Kelly through background information about herself, her professional credentials, her job description. "And in the course of your job at Cedar Grove School, did you have occasion to work with Sean Stuart?"

"Yes, his teacher asked me to observe him because she felt he wasn't talking as he should be. I recommended a language evaluation."

"Is the parent's permission needed for such an evaluation?" Sam asked.

"Yes."

"And how long after your recommendation did the evaluation take place?"

"Three days."

Sam smiled. "So Mr. Stuart gave his permission as soon as it was requested?" When she confirmed this, he said, "What were the results of your assessment?"

"The child had an expressive language delay of more than eighteen months." At Sam's request she explained the diagnosis in layman's terms, then said, "I recommended therapy, and Mr. Stuart agreed. In fact, he asked that I work with Sean daily instead of two or three times a week."

Kelly continued, delineating Sean's progress and emphasizing Grant's commitment to the child's treatment, his request that she provide intensive therapy during the summer. She sneaked an occasional glance at the jury and saw heads nodding. Even the grim-faced man's lips cracked into a half-smile when Kelly repeated some of Sean's recent utterances.

When Sam finished his questioning, Kelly allowed herself a relieved sigh, but she knew the hard part was still to come. She braced herself as Lipscomb rose.

"Miss Connery . . . it is *Miss*, isn't it?"

"Yes."

"Well, Miss Connery, in your work with youngsters such as Sean Stuart, do you attempt to involve family members in order to provide as much language stimulation as possible?"

Those were her own words. He'd undoubtedly heard them from the Hamiltons, to whom Kelly had stressed the importance of home language stimulation. "Yes, I do."

"And did you involve Mr. Stuart in your treatment?"

"Yes."

Lipscomb took a step toward her. He reminded her of a wolf on the prowl . . . and she was the prey. "Miss Connery, isn't it true that the person involved in the Stuart household was Olivia Stillwell, the housekeeper?" Before she could answer, he pressed on. "Isn't it true that the housekeeper, not Mr. Stuart, did the daily language work with Sean? Isn't it true that

Mr. Stuart is an absentee father who rarely speaks with his child?''

"Objection. Counsel is badgering the witness."

"Sustained," Judge Ritter said. "Mr. Lipscomb, please confine your cross-examination to one question at a time."

Lipscomb nodded. "Miss Connery, who was the first family member to participate in one of your sessions with Sean Stuart?''

"Olivia Stillwell, but—"

"In your position at the Stuart ranch this summer, do you have occasion to observe the comings and goings of family members?''

Kelly still smarted from Lipscomb's barrage of questions; nevertheless, she tried to remain calm. "Yes," she answered.

"Which of the family members has spent more time with Sean—the grandparents or the father?''

"Mr. Stuart is working in Boston this summer. He comes to the ranch on weekends and—"

"Answer the question, Miss Connery."

Kelly turned to the judge. His nod indicated she was to answer. All right, she would, but she'd get her two cents in at the same time. "In length of time, I'd say it was equal. Mr. Stuart spends the entire weekend with Sean. In number of occasions, the Hamiltons have visited more, but the time spent is about the same." She saw Lipscomb's scowl and Sam's smile of approval and took a breath. She'd had her say. Now maybe she could step down.

But Lipscomb wasn't ready to release her. He took a slow step closer, then another, positioning himself in front of the jury so that Kelly would have to face them when she answered. "What is your relationship with Mr. Stuart, *Miss* Connery?"

Kelly saw Grant grab Sam around the wrist, but Sam was already on his feet. "Objection," he roared. "Irrelevant."

"I'll allow it," Judge Ritter said.

Kelly stared at the judge helplessly and he gazed back, his face impassive. She'd expected this blatant probing into her private life, had told herself she was prepared, but she wasn't. She felt her face heat with embarrassment, her heartbeat accelerate with anger. The jurors, even the disinterested young man, leaned forward.

"Mr. Stuart is my employer," she stated firmly, but her voice sounded uncertain in her own ears. *They'll never believe that*, she thought, *and Lipscomb won't let it rest.*

He didn't. "Isn't it true, Miss Connery, that, in addition to being Mr. Stuart's employee, you have a *personal* relationship with him?"

"We've become friends."

Lipscomb raised a brow. "Friends?" he drawled. "Miss Connery, do you recall the week of July Fourth?" After giving her time to say she did, he went on. "Where was Sean during that week?"

"He was visiting his grandparents."

"Isn't it true, Miss Connery, that while Sean was away from the ranch, you and Mr. Stuart drove into Houston for dinner?"

"Objection!"

"Overruled," Judge Ritter said. "The witness will answer the question."

"Yes," Kelly managed. Her tongue felt thick and dry.

"And isn't it true that the two of you sat at a corner table at Brennan's holding hands, engaging in an . . . intimate conversation?"

Where had he gotten that information? Kelly's face flamed as she recalled just how intimate their dialogue had been. The jurors waited expectantly. Why not? This was better than the daily soap opera. "We were talking, yes."

"About . . speech therapy, Miss Connery?"

"Objection!"

"Sustained."

"Isn't it true, Miss Connery, that your personal relationship with Mr. Stuart precludes your being objective in this case?"

Kelly clenched her hands. Dammit, she wasn't going to sit still for this. She wouldn't let Lipscomb intimidate her by dwelling on her relationship with Grant. She looked the jurors in the eyes and spoke in a loud, clear voice. "Mr. Lipscomb, I am first and foremost Sean's speech pathologist. My personal relationships have nothing to do with my professional competence. In fact, the friendship I've developed with his father has facilitated Sean's progress. And I happen to think that Sean, like any youngster—language-delayed or not—needs all the loving interaction he can get—"

"That will be all, Miss—"

"I'm not finished," she said. "Sean needs relationships with his father *and* his grandparents *and* the housekeeper—"

"Miss Connery—"

". . . and anyone else who can provide him with love and language."

"Miss Connery, you may step down," Lipscomb said, glaring at her. Sam gave her a wide grin as she left the witness stand and walked out of the courtroom.

Grant watched her go. She was marvelous. Strong and self-assured. She'd refused to be cowed by Lipscomb. The jury, he saw, was as impressed as he was.

Next Sam called Harriet Barber from Children's Hospital, who compared Sean's current language evaluation to his initial one, then the child psychologist, whose assessment—a three-hour one—revealed Sean was a well-adjusted, happy little boy. Lipscomb tried to discredit the professionals without success.

"Grant Stuart."

He walked to the witness stand, wondering how the

jury would react to him, to his testimony. Would they see him as a fit father for Sean?"

Sam's questions were brief. "Is Sean your only child?"

"Yes, he is."

"Will you describe your relationship with your child . . . from the beginning, please."

Sam had told him to be candid, to be truthful about his parenting. He would. "Two weeks after Sean was born my wife was killed," he began in a low voice.

The judge leaned forward. "Speak up, Mr. Stuart, so the court can hear."

Grant cleared his throat and tried again. "My wife's death was a shock. I was dazed, and I felt . . ." The words stuck in his throat, but he forced them out. "I felt guilty because I hadn't driven her to the party the night she died. Olivia Stillwell, who had been with my family since I was an infant, had come to care for Sean after Claudia returned from the hospital. Olivia was there, I trusted her, and I was so overwhelmed with what had happened that I didn't have much energy left to spend on the child. And whenever I saw him, I saw his mother's face . . . Claudia's face . . . and I felt guilty all over again. My work keeps me away from home a great deal, and frankly, it was easier to let Olivia care for Sean. After a while, that became a pattern, until . . . until he began school and the teacher pointed out to me that he wasn't communicating as he should.

"I enrolled him with Ms. Connery, and she . . . well, she was pretty persistent." A couple of the jurors chuckled, and Grant smiled back at them. "Ms. Connery convinced me I had some responsibility in getting Sean to talk and I wasn't fulfilling it. I made an effort. It was halfhearted at first, but pretty soon something changed. I began to see what I'd missed. I started looking forward to spending time with Sean, talking to him, taking him fishing, reading him stories. For the first time I was acting like a father . . . and . . . and I enjoyed it.''

''And what do you want for the future?'' Sam asked.

''I want to be a full-time father. I lost three years. I can't get them back, but I don't want to lose any more time. Not a day, not a minute. I want to share Sean with his grandparents, but I want him to stay where he belongs. With me.''

''Thank you, Mr. Stuart.''

''Mr. Lipscomb?'' Judge Ritter said.

''Just a few questions, your honor.'' The attorney faced Grant. ''Mr. Stuart, were you aware that jury selection for this trial began two days ago?''

''Yes, I was.'' Grant sighed. He knew where Lipscomb was leading.

''Were you in the courtroom at that time?''

''No, I was—'' *Sam, why the hell don't you object?*

''Were you in Houston?''

Grant shook his head. ''No.''

''Thank you, Mr. Stuart.''

Judge Ritter nodded to Sam. ''Do you have further questions, Mr. Eldridge?''

Sam rose. ''Mr. Stuart, since plaintiff's attorney has brought up your failure to appear in the courtroom, would you explain to the jury the circumstances of your absence?''

''Gladly.'' He recounted his difficulties in getting to Houston; then Sam told him to step down.

Grant returned to the table, feeling drained. He'd opened up in public for the first time in his life, and it hadn't been easy. But he'd survived, he thought with relief and satisfaction.

''You may call your next witness,'' the judge told Sam.

''No more witnesses, your honor.''

''Then we'll have a brief recess and hear closing arguments. Fifteen minutes.''

''Want to stretch your legs?'' Sam asked.

Grant shook his head. He watched the jurors file past and felt the warmth of several glances. He'd won over a few of them. But what about the rest?

Closing arguments began.

Lipscomb spoke briefly but with rapier sharpness. "Here we have a man who was a disinterested husband and, by his own admission, an absentee father. He tells us he's changed, that he cares for his son, but, ladies and gentlemen, this born-again parent didn't *care* enough to arrive at the courthouse on time for jury selection, he doesn't *care* enough to curtail his business activities to spend time with his son, he doesn't *care* the way a father should. The grandparents were shocked when they learned of this sorry state of affairs. They want to take steps to give Sean Stuart the love and attention every child deserves. If *you* care, ladies and gentlemen of the jury, you'll give them . . . and Sean that opportunity."

Sam rose and walked toward the jury. He glanced at each of them in turn, then began.

"Ladies and gentlemen, my client has been honest with you. He hasn't pretended to be a model father because for three years he wasn't. He was struck by tragedy, overwhelmed, distraught, and he admits it. No, he didn't devote himself to his son, but he saw that the child had the best care available . . . from a loving housekeeper, from a fine school, from a dedicated speech pathologist. And now, Grant Stuart tells us, he's changed. He opened himself to the influence of others, he listened to what they had to say, and he learned and grew. Can anyone do more? No, he's not perfect, but who among us is? Who among us can say how he would have reacted given the same circumstances? Grant Stuart asks for the chance to raise his son, to love him. Ladies and gentlemen, I ask you to give him that chance."

The judge instructed the jury, they left the courtroom, and the waiting began.

The room they were given was small, containing a table and a couple of chairs. Sam and Kelly sat at the table; Grant stood. His chest tightened, his stomach clenched, he was cold . . . and he couldn't be still. He paced the room, from the door to the window and back, then halted to stare outside. After gazing down at the street for a full five minutes, he realized he hadn't seen a thing.

"Grant, come and sit down," Kelly said. "I'll get you some coffee."

"Caffeine's the last thing I need."

"How about a sandwich? You didn't eat breakfast. I'll bet you didn't eat lunch either."

He shook his head. He'd never be able to choke food down. "Maybe a soda."

She started for the door, then stopped. "It's going to be all right."

He met her eyes and saw that she believed it. "I hope so," he answered.

He drank his soda, and the time passed. Kelly leafed through a magazine, Sam worked a crossword puzzle, Grant continued to pace.

An hour went by, then two. What could the jury be talking about? Did they realize how painful it was to wait like this? What were they thinking, these people who held his life in the palms of their hands? He wanted to plead with them, "Give me another chance. Give me the chance to make a home for Sean."

A knock at the door brought them all to attention.

The bailiff poked his head in. "We have a verdict."

THIRTEEN

Grant was relieved; he was terrified. He followed the bailiff, wondering what he'd do if the verdict went against him. How would he survive the loss of his child?

Inside the courtroom he took his seat. With a sense of unreality, as though he were watching a television drama, he observed the events around him. Everything seemed to move in slow motion. He heard the judge ask the jury, "Ladies and gentlemen, have you reached a verdict?"

From far away, he heard, "We have, your honor."

The jury foreman handed a slip of paper to the bailiff, who carried it to the judge. The judge glanced at it and nodded.

"We find for the defendant, Grant Stuart."

For an instant, Grant sat motionless, afraid to believe the words he'd just heard, fearful he'd conjured them up out of his own longing. Then he heard the buzz of voices in the courtroom, felt Sam's hand on his shoulder. "Congratulations, pal."

"Thanks, Sam," he said hoarsely. "Thanks for everything."

"Ladies and gentlemen, thank you for your time,"

Judge Ritter said to the jury. "I'll meet with both parties tomorrow morning at ten o'clock to discuss visitation and other details."

Grant turned toward the courtroom. The jurors were leaving, some of them looking over their shoulders to smile and nod at him. Grant smiled back. These strangers, whom he would never see again, had made a vital difference in his life.

He searched for Kelly, then saw her coming toward him. As he went to meet her, the Hamiltons walked by. Joe stared past Grant, but Nancy halted and looked him straight in the eye. Her features were composed, but anger sparked in her eyes. She shot Grant a look of pure venom, then turned and marched past him.

Grant had no time to consider Nancy's response. In fact, he didn't care. His eyes were on Kelly.

She came to him, her face glowing. "Oh, Grant, I'm so glad."

"So am I." Then, heedless of the people still left in the courtroom, he pulled her into his arms. She turned her face up to him and he covered her mouth with his. He held her tight . . . in relief, in gratitude, in joy.

When he let her go, Sam stood beside them, a broad grin on his face. "Well, it's over. Want to go out and celebrate?"

Grant kept his arm around Kelly's shoulders. "Thanks, but I'd rather go back to the ranch and celebrate with Sean."

"See you in the morning then."

"Sam," Grant said, "I can't thank you enough."

"Forget it, pal. You pled your own case, and, Kelly, you were fantastic. Your testimony was the turning point. Until then, I wasn't sure we'd win." He shook hands with them, tucked his briefcase under his arm, and walked off, whistling.

"He's right," Grant said to Kelly. "You were wonderful. You won the jury over. Now, let's go home."

They spent the evening with Sean. Grant reveled in the knowledge that the child was his.

"Are you worried about tomorrow?" Kelly asked as they turned off the light in Sean's room after reading him his bedtime story.

"No, I'm sure Judge Ritter will be generous in granting visitation, and I won't object. You know I don't care for Joe and Nancy, but Sean *is* their grandchild. I can't prevent their seeing him."

"Then Sean is the real winner in this case," Kelly said. "He'll have both you and his grandparents."

Grant shook his head. "You still believe the Hamiltons are a fine, commendable couple, don't you?"

"I wouldn't say commendable, but they must have thought they could provide a good life for Sean, or they wouldn't have done this. I know they care for him. They need to be part of his life."

Grant remembered Nancy's expression that afternoon and didn't feel so sure about the Hamiltons' motives, but he let Kelly's remark pass. "We can talk about the Hamiltons another time. Right now, we have some celebrating to do . . . in private."

Kelly put out her hand. "Good idea."

The next day Grant returned to Houston, and as he had anticipated, the judge allowed the grandparents frequent access to Sean, the only stipulation being that they clear any visits with Grant beforehand.

"—and he said we'd each get Sean on alternate Christmases," Grant told Kelly when he called her from the airport.

"That sounds fair."

"I guess." He leaned against the side of the phone booth. "I told them they could have Sean this weekend. I won't be back until the weekend after. I have a lot to catch up on."

"I'll miss you," she said.

"I'll miss you, too." More than he'd imagined he

could miss anyone. "When I get back, we'll plan our island getaway."

Kelly laughed. "We'd better go soon. The summer will be over and I'll be back at work."

Grant frowned. He didn't like the idea of the summer ending, of Kelly back in her apartment instead of down the hall from him. "When does school start?"

"For Sean, August twenty-eighth; for me, a week earlier. By the way, based on Harriet's evaluation, I'll discharge Sean."

"Discharge?" He felt a twinge of fear. "Why?"

"He's made remarkable progress in such a short time. The evaluation from Children's showed he's up to age level."

"But . . but don't you think you should still see him? What if he regresses?"

She laughed. "He won't. You sound like a lot of parents. When their kids are ready for dismissal, they panic. But don't worry. I'll keep a close watch on him. Language problems can show up again when school demands change."

"Great," he muttered. "That makes me feel *real* secure."

"That's reality though. For now, Sean's doing fine. And if you need me, I'll be right there."

Not close enough, he thought. But they'd talk about that when he got back. He noticed a flight attendant heading for the jetway. Passengers were gathering their belongings. "They're about to board my plane," he said. "I'll call you tonight."

"All right. Have a good trip."

On the plane, Grant got a file from his briefcase, but he couldn't concentrate. His conversation with Kelly kept replaying in his mind.

As she'd said, the summer was ending. He dreaded the thought. She'd done so much for Sean. He couldn't imagine her not working with the child. Perhaps he could convince her to continue. No, he knew her better than that. If Kelly thought Sean didn't need further treatment, she wouldn't keep him on her rolls just to placate his father.

Was he really behaving like most parents? Getting panicked because they'd become dependent on their child's clinician? No, he decided. Sean's case was different. Kelly had been an integral part of his life for several months. Surely he'd miss her. In fact, Grant was certain her dismissing Sean would be detrimental. It would leave a huge void in Sean's life.

And in his.

He stared out the window as the plane climbed into the clouds. How could *he* get along without Kelly? She'd brought him so much. Laughter and tenderness and a new way of looking at life. No, he couldn't get along without her, and he wouldn't.

He'd never thought he'd fall in love again, but the truth was, he had. When he returned to Texas, he'd tell her how he felt. He'd ask her to marry him, to become a permanent part of his life. And he'd hope and pray she'd say yes.

Over the next days Kelly's thoughts returned to her conversation with Grant. She hated to face the end of summer, but she had to, she thought, as she took her morning horseback ride across the field with Tex trotting behind her.

Was it her imagination, or were the mornings cooler? Was a hint of autumn already in the air? Realistically, she knew that wasn't possible in Central Texas in August. But autumn was finding its way into her heart.

Soon her time at Grant's ranch would be just a memory. Sean would go back to school, to a new teacher, new experiences, continued growth. He didn't need her anymore, at least not as a speech pathologist. But he loved her, she knew that. And she loved him, too—his liveliness, his curiosity, even his stubbornness. As she'd assured Grant, she'd keep a close eye on Sean, but that wouldn't be the same as seeing him every day.

And what about Grant and their relationship? Was it an interlude, destined to fade like summer flowers? Would it die slowly until they were just acquaintances, making small talk at school functions?

"No!" she said with such vehemence that she startled the mare. No, she wouldn't let that happen. She'd resisted her attraction to Grant, gone unwillingly into his arms, but now she didn't intend to give him up. At least, not without a fight.

Of the two of them, she was the communicator. Next week when he came home again, she'd tell him how she felt. She knew the scars Claudia had inflicted were deep, but she'd shown him how to love Sean. With patience and tenderness, she would show him he could love her, too.

On Friday Joe and Nancy came to get Sean for the weekend. Kelly stared out the window as they parked their car. She wondered how her testimony at the trial would affect her relationship with them and hoped they'd understand that she'd been as objective as possible.

Nancy's first words put Kelly's fears to rest. After she'd hugged Sean and told him to get his bag, she turned to Kelly and said, "It's good to see you."

Kelly drew a breath. "I'm relieved you feel that way."

"Of course," Joe said. "We hold no grudges."

"I thought you might be upset over my testimony."

Nancy shook her head. "Not at all."

"I'm glad, because—"

Nancy held up her hand. "You don't have to explain yourself to us, Kelly."

"No, indeed," Joe agreed. "You did what you had to do, and we understand completely."

Kelly frowned, not sure they did understand. She

would have asked what Joe's comment meant, but Sean came into the room, struggling with a half-zipped duffel bag full of clothing, his ever-present teddy bear, and a box spilling over with toys that he dropped in the middle of the room. "My bucket falled out," he complained.

"You won't need the bucket at Grandma and Granddad's," Kelly told him, leaning over to pick it up.

"Yes, I do. I need it. I wanna dig in the sand," Sean insisted.

Kelly turned to Nancy and shrugged. "Last time he was here Grant talked about going to the beach, and Sean's been asking to go ever since. We've read every beach book we could find."

Nancy ruffled Sean's hair. "You bring the bucket next time, honey. We'll spend a whole day at the beach." She forestalled any further argument by saying, "Come, Sean. Let Granddad help you and we'll get started." Then she reached into her bag, took out an envelope, and turned to Kelly. "We have something for you—just a token of our appreciation for all you've done with Sean."

Kelly opened the envelope. A cashier's check for ten thousand dollars! She stared in shock. "I . . . thank you, but . . ."

"It's for your school," Joe explained, beaming at her.

And for what else? What strings were attached? What were the Hamiltons trying to buy? They'd just been through an ugly custody battle. Perhaps they saw their gift to her as a way to use her as an intermediary with Grant. Should she take the money? *Yes,* she decided. Whatever the Hamiltons' reasons for giving it, the money would be put to good use. She shook off her negative thoughts. "I don't know how to thank you."

"Just keep doing good work."

"I promise you, I will."

"Good," Nancy said. "We expect to see your school in operation when we visit next summer."

When they left, Kelly sank onto the couch and stared again at the check. Enough money to turn The Language Center from a dream to solid reality! As soon as the house was available, she'd make a down payment, and now she'd have enough to furnish it in style.

Kelly wanted to cry; she wanted to shout. Instead, she clutched the check to her chest and danced around the room. When she was so out of breath she couldn't move, she flopped down on the couch again, shut her eyes, and imagined the school fully equipped, brimming with children and staff. Every detail went through her mind, everything down to the sign in the front yard. She sat up, read the check again to make sure she wasn't hallucinating, then ran into the hall to call Marla and tell her the good news. "Guess what! The Hamiltons have turned fairy godmother and underwritten The Language Center!"

"Fantastic!" Marla cried. "I'm breaking out the champagne for a long distance toast!"

Kelly wondered what Grant would think of the check. She wondered if the Hamiltons' generosity would soften his angry feelings or fuel his suspicions.

When she spoke to him that night, his reaction was typical. He only mumbled, "I see."

"I know how you feel," Kelly said, "but try to be positive. Maybe Joe and Nancy are trying to build bridges through Sean."

"We'll see," he said, and she could tell he didn't want to discuss it any further.

Sean returned from his visit to the Hamiltons on Sunday evening, and the next few days passed quietly. Wednesday Grant phoned to say that the president of a shoe store he was negotiating with would be in Boston and would keep him busy Thursday and Friday until late evening, so he wouldn't be in until Saturday afternoon. Kelly was disappointed, but she realized how much time he'd lost because of the trial.

Sean was not so understanding. He stuck out his lip. "Why Daddy not coming?"

"He has some work to do. He'll be here Saturday. That's only one more day to wait."

"I wanna go fishing."

Ah, that was it. "I'll take you."

"Now?"

"Tomorrow." Kelly wasn't a fisherman. Maybe, she decided, if she postponed the fishing trip, Sean would forget about it.

On Thursday morning Nancy called just as they were finishing breakfast. "The Alley Theater has a wonderful children's play. I'd like to take Sean this afternoon."

"Sounds great," Kelly said, pleased that this would postpone her fishing trip even further. "Sean is disappointed that Grant won't be here until Saturday. This will give him something to do."

"That's my thought exactly," Nancy agreed. "We're looking forward to spending the rest of the week with our boy. And, Kelly, I need a favor. Joe had a business appointment, and my car is in the shop. Would you mind driving Sean into Houston?"

"Not at all."

"Thanks. Don't forget his teddy bear and his bucket."

Kelly loaded Sean, the bear, the bucket, the Ninja Turtles and their airplane, a book, and clothes into the car, and they set off for Houston. "Maybe Grant can pick him up Saturday on his way in from the airport," she suggested when she dropped Sean off at the townhouse the Hamiltons had leased for the summer.

Nancy hesitated. "Maybe. We'll work something out."

Kelly left Sean and his grandfather unpacking Turtle

figures and headed for Marla's. When she arrived, Walter ambled into the living room. He paused, eyed her disdainfully, and strolled off, tail held high. "He thinks I abandoned him," Kelly said.

Marla snorted. "That's his personality. Aloof, uncommunicative males seem attracted to you. And vice versa."

"You're right. The kind of males who are warm-hearted and cuddly beneath their cold exteriors."

"Cuddly, huh?" Marla said. "You'll have to tell me more about that over lunch."

They indulged their appetite for Mexican food, then strolled through the Galleria looking at the new fall fashions. Afterward Kelly drove back to the ranch, eagerly awaiting Saturday and the arrival of her favorite aloof-on-the-outside-but-cuddly-on-the-inside male.

When she heard his car pull up, she flew downstairs and out onto the porch and flung herself into his arms.

"Mmm," he murmured. "What a nice welcome."

Kelly stepped back and laughed up at him, then looked toward the car. Grant turned, holding the door halfway open. "Where's Sean?" they said at the same time.

Kelly frowned. "Didn't you pick him up?"

"No," Grant said. "Where is he? Over at the Eldridges'?"

Kelly felt a sudden chill. "N . . . no. He's with his grandparents."

The screen door slammed shut. "He's *where*?"

"At . . . at Joe and Nan . . ." She stared at him in confusion. "Didn't you know?"

"No, I didn't." His eyes flashed.

"But they said—" Actually, Kelly realized, they *hadn't* said they'd checked with Grant. She'd just assumed they had.

"They have a helluva nerve, coming down here and picking him up," Grant snarled, striding into the house and picking up the phone. "They can bring him back right now."

Kelly put her hand on his arm. "Ah, actually they didn't come down here. They called and I drove him to Houston."

"You . . . drove . . . him . . . to . . . Houston. Without bothering to find out whether they'd gotten permission to have him?"

"They implied they'd spoken to you." At least, she'd *thought* they had. "Anyway, you said the judge had given them unlimited visitation."

"I said frequent visitation, *with* permission." He yanked the receiver out of its cradle and started jabbing in the Hamiltons' number.

"Grant, what's the harm? They wanted to take him to the Alley, and yesterday you weren't here, so they kept him a little longer. They'll be leaving in a couple of weeks, and I'm sure they want to spend as much time with Sean as they can."

Grant muttered something sharp and angry.

"Grant," Kelly pleaded, "aren't you overreacting? Why not give them the pleasure of a day with Sean now? After they're gone, he'll be all yours."

Grant sighed. "I suppose you're right." He replaced the receiver and went outside to retrieve the bag he'd dropped when Kelly had lunged into his arms. When he returned, he asked, "When did they say they'd bring him back?"

"I told them you'd be here this afternoon, so they'll probably show up any time now. Why don't you put your things away and I'll fix us some iced tea?"

Grant went upstairs and returned a few minutes later. He'd put on a pair of khaki cutoffs, a dark brown T-shirt, and a pair of sneakers that made him look casual and relaxed, but Kelly could see he wasn't. Despite agreeing that he'd overreacted about Sean, he couldn't shed his edginess. As he sipped his tea, he kept turning toward the window at the slightest sound. When Tex began barking, Grant got up and went to the front door. A few minutes later, he returned, looking anxious. "Where the hell are they?"

"Probably stuck in weekend traffic," Kelly said. "Come on. Let's walk down to the stable."

"Too hot."

"How about a swim then?" she suggested.

"No, thanks. You go ahead."

Kelly sighed, half in exasperation, half in understanding. "Grant, if you're going to stew about this all afternoon, why don't you go ahead and call Joe and Nancy? I'm sure they'll have a reasonable explanation."

"All right." Kelly followed him and watched as he dialed and waited for an answer, pacing back and forth. Finally, he hung up and shook his head. "They're not home."

"See? I'm sure they're on their way." They both turned at the sound of an automobile and hurried to the door.

But instead of the Hamiltons, they saw Lynn Eldridge and her two children. "Hi," she called, coming up the walk. "I thought I'd see if Sean would like to come by for a swim."

"He's not here," Grant said.

"Visiting his grandparents?"

"Yeah," he replied gruffly.

Lynn turned to Kelly. "Is Grant in one of his moods?"

"This isn't funny," Grant snapped. "Joe and Nancy took Sean without permission, and they're late bringing him back."

Lynn's face sobered. "Shall I tell Sam when he gets in?" When Grant nodded, she continued, "Give him a call. He'll be in around six." She glanced back at her car. "I'd better get these two rascals home before they demolish the backseat. See you."

As she drove off, Grant stalked back to the phone. "Still no answer."

"Because they're somewhere between here and Houston. Come on. Let's go for that swim. You'll feel better."

But the swim didn't serve its purpose. Grant swam laps again and again. As she watched him, Kelly felt a wave of guilt. How could she have been so easily persuaded to let Sean go to the Hamiltons'? Why hadn't she checked with Grant? Supervising Sean was her responsibility. Soon she found herself as uptight as Grant. What was taking Joe and Nancy so long? Had they misunderstood when Grant was arriving? Or had something happened to them?

Finally Grant emerged from the water. He gave himself a swipe with a towel, then started for the house. "I'm calling them again."

Again, there was no answer.

"I'm going to notify the highway patrol," Grant said. He did, but an hour went by with no report of an accident.

Thirty minutes later the phone rang. Grant stopped pacing the living room and grabbed the receiver. "Hello."

Kelly again followed him into the hall. She'd like nothing better than to hear him raking Joe or Nancy over the coals.

Instead, he said, "Yeah, Sam. Thanks for calling. Yeah, they took him without my consent." He listened a moment, then said, "I'm not as concerned right now with consequences as I am with finding them. They don't answer their phone. I've alerted the highway patrol, but so far, they haven't come up with anything. I've got to hang up now. I'll call you when I hear."

"You know what I think," Kelly said. "They've probably gone out for the day, maybe to the zoo, and they've let the time get away from them. No, wait. I remember now. You know how Sean's been talking about going to the beach? They told me to bring his bucket. I'll bet they've gone to Galveston.''

"I guess you're right." Grant seemed relieved for a moment, then anger reasserted itself. "They have no business taking off like that," he growled. "Next week we're going back before the judge. They can abide by the terms of the agreement or forget about seeing Sean. And I'm driving into Houston now and telling them what I think."

"But they're not home," Kelly protested.

"I'll park outside and wait for them."

"What if they decide to come straight here after the beach?"

He sighed. "Yeah, they might."

"Everything'll be fine, you'll see," Kelly said, as much to reassure herself as to placate Grant.

Olivia poked her head into the living room. "Dinner's on the table."

They filled the housekeeper in on the situation, then went into the breakfast room. Grant ate little; Kelly pushed her food around on her plate. Finally, they gave up pretending to eat and returned to the living room. During the interminable evening, Kelly tried to lose herself in a book, but she looked up at every sound from outside, at every movement from Grant.

He took a stack of papers from his briefcase and began reading them, but Kelly saw he couldn't concentrate. He checked his watch every few minutes and kept pinching the bridge of his nose.

"Have a headache?" She went to him and massaged the back of his neck. "Better?"

"Yeah." He rose. "It's after eleven. I'm going to bed. If Sean's not here in the morning, I'll drive into Houston—" His eyes narrowed. "—whether it's over-reacting or not."

Kelly watched him stalk out of the living room. For the first time since they'd been together, he hadn't asked her to join him, and tonight she didn't feel like taking the initiative. As his footsteps died away, she thought ruefully that this was the night she'd planned to tell Grant she loved him.

FOURTEEN

Kelly awoke at first light. Her head ached and her mouth felt fuzzy. She'd barely slept. Every few minutes she'd been up looking out the window, scanning the dark driveway, hoping in vain to catch sight of headlights. She'd been half tempted to drive into Houston herself, confront the Hamiltons, and bring Sean home. She'd squelched that idea, knowing Grant wouldn't have appreciated her intervention at this point.

Now she strained to hear if he was moving around. No sound came from the hallway, and she slipped out of bed, pulled on a pair of jeans and a T-shirt, and tiptoed out of her room on bare feet. She didn't want to wake Grant—she was sure his night had been worse than hers.

She went downstairs and plugged in the coffee maker, then sat at the table and let her head fall forward onto her arms. Her eyes closed and she drifted back into sleep until the sound of footsteps awakened her. Grant entered the breakfast room. "Good morning," Kelly said, her voice scratchy with exhaustion. "I won't ask how you slept, only *if* you slept."

"I didn't." He poured a cup of coffee for Kelly, then filled a mug for himself. "I'm going to drive into Houston."

The coffee reviving her, Kelly said, "I'll go with you."

Grant shook his head. "If they bring him home—"

"Olivia will be here."

As if the sound of her name had summoned her, Olivia came out of the kitchen, clad in an ancient-looking bathrobe, her face bare of makeup, her hair in rollers. "Have you heard anything, Grant?" she asked. Deep circles under her eyes attested to a night as sleepless as Kelly's and Grant's.

"Nothing," Grant said.

"We're leaving for Houston in a little while," Kelly said.

Grant frowned at her. "Kelly, I don't wan—"

"I'm going," she said. He needed her along as a buffer. As upset as he was, she shuddered to think what he might say—or do—if he faced Joe and Nancy alone. Aside from that, he needed her support . . . and her love to get him through this.

"All right," Grant said, scowling again. "I don't want to waste time arguing. Let's get started."

"You need breakfast first," Olivia said. "I know neither of you had a wink of sleep, and you're not leaving without food."

In a few minutes, she brought them plates of scrambled eggs and toast. "How about you?" Kelly asked her. "Where's your breakfast?"

"I'm not hungry," she confessed. "I'm too worried."

After halfhearted attempts to eat, they left the house. Silent and stony-faced, Grant sped down the highway.

They drove east into the sun, which shone from a clear blue sky. Outside the car was a perfect summer morning. Inside, it might have been mid-winter.

Grant kept the speedometer at eighty until they reached the outskirts of Houston. When they arrived at the Hamiltons' townhouse, he parked across the street, then sat for a moment, gripping the steering wheel.

Kelly touched his arm. "It's going to be all right."

He didn't answer. He'd shut her out again. Yes, she understood how angry and upset he was, but was this how he reacted to every crisis, barricading himself behind a wall of silence? She had to pierce that armor. "Listen to me. I love Sean, and I'm worried, too, now." When he didn't answer, she gripped his hand. "Talk to me, Grant."

He turned to her, his eyes bleak, his mouth grim. "Talk's cheap."

"But it helps."

He shook his head, but he turned his hand over and grasped hers. He needed her, Kelly realized, even if he couldn't voice that need. She wrapped her arms around him and they held each other. After a few minutes, Grant pulled away and shoved the door open. "What we need now is action." He started across the street.

Kelly followed, hurrying to keep up with his longer strides. A man two houses down came out in his robe to pick up the Sunday paper. He eyed them curiously.

Grant reached the door of the townhouse before Kelly and punched the bell once, twice, then again. No one answered.

"Damn!" he muttered and gave the doorbell another jab. After another moment of fruitless waiting, he said, "Stay here. I'm going around the back."

Kelly remained on the steps, staring at the heavy wooden door, praying it would open. Five minutes passed before Grant reappeared. "No one's there."

They returned to the car and waited. Kelly made no attempt to talk to Grant, knowing he'd respond in monosyllables. Instead, she kept her hand on his, communicating her support.

She noticed the neighbor who'd come outside earlier watching them through his window. "Maybe that man knows the Hamiltons," she suggested. "He might be able to tell us where they've gone."

Grant nodded and got out again. As he headed

toward the man's townhouse, the door opened. "You looking for someone?"

"Yes," Grant answered.

The two met halfway up the walk. Kelly couldn't hear what they said, but she saw Grant gesture toward the Hamiltons' house, saw the man shake his head and say something. She couldn't see Grant's reaction; his back was toward her. They stood talking for a few minutes, and then Grant followed the man into his house.

Kelly waited, wondering what the man had told Grant. Had something happened to Sean? No, the Hamiltons would have called. Could Joe be ill, or Nancy? Kelly shifted in her seat, then saw the door open.

Grant appeared, said something over his shoulder, and strode down the walk, his face a thundercloud. He got into the car, slammed the door, and sped into the street, tires screeching.

Surely the worst had happened. *Damn him for his silence*. "What is it?" Kelly demanded.

"They're gone" was the terse reply. "Disappeared. Vanished. And they took Sean with them."

Kelly stared at him in dazed confusion. "What do you mean? Gone where?"

"They moved out—lock, stock, and barrel."

"Wh . . . when?"

"Yesterday morning. The neighbor saw the rental company pick up their furniture." The car careened around the corner and up the freeway entrance ramp.

She couldn't believe what she'd heard, didn't want to believe it. "How could that be? The neighbor must be mistaken."

"No. He gave me the number of the leasing agent for the townhouses. She confirmed it."

"But . . . but the phone's still connected."

"Sure. They're clever. They left it on. What's a little added phone bill when you're planning a kidnapping?"

"Kidnapping!" Kelly's heart seemed to stop. Her

limbs turned ice cold at the sound of the word. But a kidnapping was what Grant had described. For once words failed her. She sat silently, in shock, as the car wove in and out of traffic, pushing the speed limit. "Grant, where are we going?"

"To my office. To call Sam, the police, the FBI, or whoever it takes to get Sean back again."

Kelly sat across the desk from Grant as he spoke with Sam on the phone. He hadn't said another word to her after he'd announced his intention to go to his office. Mute with shock herself, Kelly hadn't attempted any further conversation. She'd followed him into the high-rise building and into the twentieth-floor office that looked exactly as she had once imagined his work environment—sleek, subdued, and impersonal.

As soon as they arrived, he'd called the Houston police and given them descriptions of Sean and his grandparents. Though he didn't relay the officer's response to Kelly, she guessed from Grant's scowl that the man hadn't been optimistic.

Now Grant growled at Sam, "Distributing pictures to the airlines may tell us where they've headed, but it's too slow. I want results." Grant listened, then said, "A detective? Is he good? More to the point, is he fast?" Apparently Sam said yes, for Grant grabbed a pencil. "Give me his name and number.'

Kelly watched Grant scribble the information on a memo pad. This couldn't be happening. It was a nightmare. Surely she'd wake up any minute, hear Sean at her door asking her to read him a story. But she knew the situation was all too real.

Grant punched in a phone number and drummed his fingers on the desk. "Let me speak to Theodore Grimsley." He listened, then snapped, "Yes, I know it's Sunday. I don't care. This is an emergency." He gave his name and number and hung up.

"Theodore?" Kelly murmured. *Theodore* didn't

sound like a detective. Private investigators were named Jake or Max. Theodore, with Grimsley after it, sounded like . . . a butler. She suppressed an urge to laugh, realizing she was close to hysteria.

They waited silently until the phone rang. Grant grabbed it. "Grant Stuart," he barked. The caller must have been Theodore, for Grant gave a rundown of Sean's disappearance. When he hung up, he glanced at Kelly as if aware of her presence for the first time since they'd arrived at his office. "He's coming over."

Theodore's appearance belied his name. He might have stepped out of a detective series on TV. Tall, solid muscled, and with shaggy hair and piercing eyes, he sported a tattoo on one arm—a heart with "Love Me, Baby" beneath it. Theodore looked as though he could tough it out with the best . . . or worst of the world.

He presented both Grant and Kelly with business cards listing him as Theodore Anthony Grimsley, president of A-One Investigations, then said, "You can call me Tag."

Kelly nodded. She had a feeling anyone who called him Theodore after that would get punched in the face.

Tag sat down and said, "Okay, tell me everything about the kid and the grandparents. Don't leave anything out. Even if it seems unimportant to you, it could be the one critical detail. Got it?" He took a tape recorder out of his battered briefcase and set it on the desk. "Beats taking notes," he explained, then slouched in the chair.

Tag's lazy posture was a sham, Kelly decided. Not a detail escaped him as she and Grant recited the events that had led up to the weekend. He stopped them frequently, asking for more information, insisting they remember all particulars that could have the slightest bearing on Sean's disappearance.

"—and so you brought him into Houston, Miz Connery," he said. "What did you pack?"

"Enough clothing for a couple of days, his teddy bear . . . and, oh, yes, his bucket."

"Why a bucket?"

"He'd been wanting to go to the beach. Nancy said next time they might take him. But she didn't say they were going, just said not to forget the bucket."

"Okay," Tag said. "Why did you drive him?"

Kelly thought for a moment. "Um, Nancy said her car was in the shop and Joe had an appointment."

"Okay. Everything look normal at their house?"

"I . . . I don't know," Kelly said. "I'd never been there before."

"Well, think about it, Miz Connery. Did it look bare? Like they were getting ready to move out?"

Kelly shut her eyes, trying to remember what she'd seen. "It looked . . . normal to me. I didn't see many personal things around, but they were just leasing for the summer."

"See any suitcases?"

"No, I'm sure of that."

"New clothes for the kid?"

Had she seen any? "No . . . wait, there was a bag from Neiman Marcus on the coffee table, but I didn't see what was in it."

Tag made a note to contact Neiman Marcus. He questioned Grant about his relationship with the Hamiltons, got their address in San Francisco and the names of Joe's company and business partner.

"What kind of business?" Tag asked.

"Importing. Joe has been based in Japan for four y—" He went white. "You don't think they've taken Sean to Japan?"

Tag shook his head. "No chance. Unless the kid carries a passport along with his teddy bear. Takes a parent to apply for a passport."

Grant took a long breath and leaned back.

Tag turned back to Kelly. "Unlike Mr. Stuart here, you seem to have a close relationship with these people.

Any reason you might be cooperating with them on this kidnapping?"

Kelly's mouth dropped open. "Me? Cooperating?"

Grant half rose from his chair. "Listen, Grimsley, she didn't have anything to do with this."

Tag raised a hand. "Whoa there, Mr. Stuart. I'm just asking. It's what you're hiring me for, right?" He turned his attention back to Kelly, who still sat stunned. "Well, Miz Connery? Any reason you'd want to see the grandparents get the kid? They offer you higher pay to work with him, maybe?"

Kelly swallowed her anger and reminded herself Theodore Anthony Grimsley was indeed doing what he was paid to. "No. Number one, I wouldn't have accepted such a job had it been offered, and number two, Sean doesn't need my services anymore. I'm planning to discharge him at the end of the summer."

"Okay," Tag said. "Let's go on." He questioned them for another full hour, then rose and stretched. "Get me some pictures of the boy and the grandparents."

Grant pulled a recent snapshot of Sean from his wallet. Kelly remembered when Grant had taken it. Sean was in the pool, beaming with pride at having paddled all the way across for the first time. Was that less than a month ago? Would they ever see Sean again?

"I have some better pictures at the house. I can probably dig up one of the Hamiltons, too. You'll have them in an hour," Grant said.

"Good. Meanwhile, I'll run background checks on the grandparents. Don't worry, Mr. Stuart. I'll find your kid."

But he didn't.

Three days passed, then four. Four days of dead ends, of dashed hopes. Four days of articles in the morning newspaper: DEVELOPER'S SON DISAPPEARS. GRANDPARENTS SUSPECTED IN KIDNAPPING.

Grant was certain he was going mad. He'd never felt so angry or so damn helpless in his life. Sean and the Hamiltons had disappeared.

They'd taken a plane to Phoenix, that much Grimsley had discovered. There, they'd vanished. They weren't in San Francisco, and Joe's partner swore they hadn't contacted him, but Grant wasn't so sure about that. Grimsley wasn't either; he'd informed Grant he'd be checking out the California angle. Grant could do nothing but wait.

He'd stayed in Houston, leaving the Boston development to his associates. He'd tried halfheartedly to manage the Houston end of the business, without success. How could you think about business when your child was missing?

At least he'd had Kelly to lean on. She'd stayed with him at his Houston home, holding him through the bleak, empty hours of night, the time when he was most afraid he'd never see Sean again. She'd been a tower of strength, even though he knew she was as worried and frightened as he was. She'd even put up with his silence. He wondered what he'd have done without her.

And yet . . .

And yet, something disturbed him. Though he'd steadfastly pushed the thought aside, something had nagged at him since his first meeting with Grimsley, something the detective had said . . . to Kelly.

Any reason you might be cooperating with them on this kidnapping? Kelly had been astounded at the question, and Grant had been so angry he'd been tempted to deck Grimsley. Of course, they'd both assured Grimsley there was no way Kelly could be mixed up in this. Not Kelly, who'd singlehandedly brought him and Sean together. Not Kelly, who'd become essential to his life. After a marriage made in hell, he'd finally found a woman he could love and trust.

And yet, something continued to prey on his mind. Something about Kelly and the Hamiltons.

Grimsley fueled the half-formed suspicion during their daily phone conversation. "Could be someone's leaking details of our investigation to the grandparents, keeping them a step ahead of me." Tag paused to let that sink in, then said, "It's gotta be somebody who knows as much as you and me."

Grant laughed that off. "Nobody knows as much as we do, except Sam, who did his damnedest to get me custody and who dislikes the Hamiltons besides."

"What about your . . . friend?"

"Kelly?" He tried to laugh that off, too. "Don't you trust anyone, Grimsley?"

"Nope, not even you, Mr. Stuart. For all I know, you could have some crazy scheme up your a—, up your sleeve, and be hiding the boy in a closet. I'd say chances are pretty slim on that one. But your friend now, she was pretty thick with the grandparents. Give it some thought."

"I don't have to," Grant said. "It makes no sense for Kelly . . ." Grimsley waited, but Grant didn't finish. Because what crossed his mind was something he wasn't ready to share with the detective. Because now the nagging thought he'd suppressed for the last four days pushed to the forefront of his mind and confronted him squarely. Ten thousand dollars. The Hamiltons' donation for Kelly's school.

"Hit on something?" Grimsley asked.

"No, nothing." He and Grimsley hung up, and Grant remained at his desk, staring into space and thinking.

Perhaps he should talk to Kelly about the check; then he could get it off his mind. She believed in communication. Maybe the time had come for him to try it, too.

That evening they sat half watching a medical drama on television. "Do you mind if I change channels?" Kelly asked.

Grant nodded. "Every time the ambulance pulls up to that emergency entrance, I worry if Sean—"

"Me, too."

"Turn it off," Grant said. "I want to talk to you." As he watched the screen go blank, he took a deep breath and felt his heart jump the way it had when he was a kid about to dive off the high board. He didn't want to broach this subject with Kelly, but he had to know.

She turned to him, and he said, "I want you to go over last weekend again, see if you missed anything—something Nancy said, something you saw."

She shook her head and he heard a weary sigh. "Grant, we've gone over this again and again. I've told you everything that happened. I didn't leave anything out."

Granted nodded. "They took a chance by not calling me for permission. You might not have let Sean go."

"I've asked myself a hundred times why I didn't question them. I was sure they'd called you. After all, they did the week before. And Nancy seemed to know you wouldn't be back until Saturday. Now, of course, I realize *I* told her that, and she only echoed what I said." She stared down at her hands for a moment, then said, "But even if they'd called you and you'd said no, that wouldn't have stopped them from taking Sean."

He nodded. She was right. "Why were you so sure they were going to bring him back?"

"Why wouldn't I be? They'd always brought him back before."

That made sense, at least on the surface. "I should have gone after him immediately."

"I should have let you. But I thought you were overreacting."

"Why?"

"Because of the trial. Because you don't like the Hamiltons." She raised pain-filled eyes to his.

Still, he continued to probe. "*You* like the Hamiltons."

"*Liked*. I was wrong. They aren't much different from their daughter, are they? Wanting their way, no matter what." She turned away from Grant and stared out the window.

"They gave you a check."

She nodded, her eyes still on the scene outside. "I guess that colored my opinion of them, too."

"What are you going to do with the money, Kelly?" he asked.

"I don't know. I've thought of . . ." She turned back to him, stared into his eyes, and read the question in his mind. "What are you asking me, Grant?" she snapped.

"I asked what you're planning to do with the money."

"No," she said, narrowing her eyes. "That's not what you're asking, is it? Is it?" she repeated.

"I want you to tell me the ten thousand dollars didn't have anything to do with what happened last weekend."

Kelly's face went pale. "How can you say that?" she said, her voice shaking. "How can you even think it?"

"I don't think—"

"Yes, you do, or you wouldn't have said what you did." Her eyes swam with tears. "You think they bought me, don't you? You think I was in on their plans, that I took Sean to them on purpose. Don't you?"

"I want you to tell me it's not true," he muttered.

Her hands trembling, Kelly stood. "No, Grant, I won't tell you that. You had no right to ask it, or even think it." She took a step toward the door, then stopped and turned to him. "I *love* Sean. And, until two minutes ago, I loved you, too."

She started for the door, and Grant got up. "Kelly—"

"I'm leaving." He took a step toward her and put out his hand in supplication. "Don't try to stop me," she said, the tears clogging her voice, "and don't say anything. I'll be out of here in fifteen minutes."

She ran from the room and he heard her footsteps on the stairs. He sat down and put his head in his hands. In a few minutes, he heard Kelly come downstairs, heard the front door open and shut, and listened to the sound of her car as she drove away.

He knew he should go after her, but he couldn't seem to pull himself out of the chair. Not now, not with all that was going on in his life. He'd hurt her and he didn't know the words to make things right. He'd blurted out his thoughts, but they'd come out all wrong. His one attempt at communication had failed. That jump off the high board had ended in a belly flop, and he didn't know if he could take another.

Kelly picked up the telephone and dialed Grant's house. She'd spoken to Olivia both days since she'd come home, each morning waiting until she was certain Grant had left for his office. So far, there was no word of Sean.

"Stuart residence."

"Olivia, this is Kelly. Any news?"

"Nothing. The detective's going to California tomorrow to see if he can hunt them down."

"How's Grant?"

Olivia sighed. "He's in terrible shape. Since you left, he's walked around like a lost soul. Kelly," she hesitated a moment, then continued, "I know it's none of my business, but won't you come back? Grant needs you."

"He may need me," Kelly agreed, "but he doesn't trust me."

"Why, what makes you say a thing like that? Of course, he trusts you."

"No." Kelly found herself telling the housekeeper all that had happened the other evening.

"Wh . . . why that— I'd like to take him over my knee like I did when he was little," Olivia sputtered. Then she added, "You know he didn't mean those words."

"Maybe not, but he said them."

"He's just so torn now, he doesn't know what he's saying," Olivia went on. "Once Sean's home again, you two will work things out." But Kelly heard a break in the older woman's voice, as if she'd given up hope of Sean's coming home again.

"Tag will find him," she assured Olivia. Then, unable to control her own voice any longer, she said, "I have to go. I'll call you tomorrow."

Kelly hung up and sat staring at the receiver. Walter strolled by and she called to him, but he ignored her. When she'd picked him up from Marla the day before yesterday, he'd acted as if she were a stranger and he'd continued giving her the silent treatment, except for mealtimes, of course. "You don't trust me either, do you?" she called after him. "You think I'm going to leave you again."

Walter responded with a flick of his tail.

"All right, be that way. Both of you," she added, including Grant.

Needing to keep busy, she filled a plastic bottle and misted the plants she'd brought home from Marla's, then set about repotting the schefflera, which had outgrown its container over the summer.

How could he have thought she was collaborating with the Hamiltons? Hadn't she shown him by everything she'd done all summer how much she cared for Sean . . . and for him? She'd testified before a jury, made her life an open book to be pored over by gossip mongers, defended Grant in court, stood by him, loved him. But it hadn't been enough.

Was he so scarred from his marriage that he could

never trust again? Had Claudia's betrayal made him unable to accept what Kelly had offered? Hadn't her love healed his wounds? With each question, she stabbed the soil with her trowel. She'd wanted to believe it had, but perhaps she hadn't given him enough time. Maybe if the kidnapping hadn't happened, things would have been different.

"If," she muttered. What good was "if"? She couldn't go back and change events.

One thing Grant had been right about, she acknowledged, was Joe and Nancy. Self-centered, devious, uncaring—just like Claudia. Why hadn't she seen the signs? That first day they'd met, when Nancy had demanded she make time for them the next afternoon. Nancy's insistence that plans be altered to suit her and Joe. The indications were there, but Kelly hadn't noticed.

She patted the last bit of soil into place and stood back to check the schefflera. Then she looked around for something else to do, something that required a lot of energy and not much thought. She decided to scour the bathtub. Nothing more mindless and energetic than that.

As she scrubbed though, she couldn't keep her thoughts from returning to Grant. By getting involved with him, she'd managed to violate every one of Connery's Commandments, even the third and most important one, which she'd composed as she left Grant's house: Never fall in love with a client. But she had, and look where it had gotten her—down on her knees, scouring the tub.

When Kelly had mentioned her broken rules to Marla, her friend had insisted that Grant's being a client was coincidental. "He was the wrong man for you," she'd said. When Kelly tried to argue, Marla shook her head. "He's just like he seems on the surface—cold."

Funny though, even now in the depths of her despair, Kelly didn't buy that. Wary, yes, but she still believed

Grant's coldness was a shield against vulnerability. And in her heart of hearts, in spite of everything that had happened between them, she still loved him.

Kelly stood and surveyed the bathtub. The porcelain sparkled like new, but she'd had enough of cleaning. What to do now? Good thing school was starting. She'd spend the rest of the morning going through her materials. That would keep her occupied for a while.

She went to the spare bedroom, which she used as an office, opened a file drawer, and began thumbing through a folder of food pictures. "Fruits, vegetables, desserts—"

The telephone rang.

Kelly dropped the folder and dashed to answer, wondering as she did each time it rang if Grant were calling. "Don't get your hopes up," she muttered and picked up the receiver. "Hello."

"Kelly."

Her legs went weak and she sat down abruptly. The caller didn't have to identify himself. She recognized the voice immediately. It was Joe Hamilton.

FIFTEEN

"Where are you?" Kelly managed to whisper. She seemed to have run out of air.

"I can't tell you that."

"Is . . . is Sean with you? Is he all right?"

"Yes, of course he's with us. And, no, he isn't all right. That's what I called you about."

She clutched the receiver. "Wh . . . what's wrong with him?"

"Don't worry. He isn't sick," Joe said, "but he's quit talking. I want you to tell us what to do."

Kelly let out the breath she'd been holding. At least he wasn't ill. The talking could be handled, but first Sean had to come home. "If you want my help, tell me where you are."

"Not yet."

"Then tell me what's wrong."

"I told you. He won't talk," Joe replied.

"Has he stopped altogether?"

"No, he tells us when he wants something, but he won't join in a conversation the way he used to. He won't play much either; just sits with his bear."

"He's upset," Kelly said. "You have to bring him home."

"His home's here," he answered implacably.

"Where, Joe?"

"With us. You've always worked so well with Sean. Nancy and I want you to come out here and stay with us for a while, get him talking again."

"How can I come if I don't know where you are?"

"We'll talk about that later. What I want to know is when you can come. We'll pay you double what you got from Grant, far more than you get at Cedar Grove."

Kelly wished she knew the appropriate way to deal with the situation. Should she agree, find out where Sean was, and send Tag after him? What would a psychologist do? Since she wasn't an expert, she'd have to go with what she knew and pray it was right. "No, I won't come."

"We'll pay you triple your salary at Grant's."

Grant was right. The Hamiltons thought they could buy anything, including her. "Money isn't the issue."

"If something else is, name it. We'll work it out."

"I can't help you."

"Why not? You've done a magnificent job with Sean up till now. If anyone can get him out of this slump, you can."

Kelly chose her words carefully. The last thing she wanted was to antagonize Joe. "I'm not a psychiatrist, but as a language specialist, I can tell you that when a child regresses suddenly like this, the cause is probably emotional." She wanted to say flat out that Joe and Nancy had caused Sean's regression by removing the child from his home, but instead she tried to be tactful. "Sean has undergone drastic changes in the last week. He's telling you by his silence that he can't cope with them. Bring him back, Joe. Please."

"I'll call you back."

"Wait—" But before she could say any more, the line went dead.

"Oh, my God. What now?" She got up to pace the floor. Should she call Grant? No, she decided. Their relationship was too strained. Besides, she didn't want to get Grant's hopes up, then find that Joe wouldn't cooperate. She thought of contacting Tag, then realized the detective was on his way to San Francisco. She'd call Sam.

When she heard his voice on the phone, she knew she'd made the right decision. Sam was cool-headed and quick-thinking. She told him about her conversation with Joe, and he said, "You handled it just right. I wish you'd gotten him to tell you where they are, but you can do that on the next call."

"*If* there's a next call," Kelly said.

"There will be," Sam assured her.

"I'm not leaving this apartment until I hear from him."

"Okay, now here's what you tell him—"

After she finished talking to Sam, Kelly went back into her office. She wasn't hungry, she couldn't sit still, and her tub was squeaky clean. She'd have to make do with her therapy materials until Joe called back. But she found herself stopping every few minutes to look at her watch or pace into the living room and glare at the silent telephone.

Two hours later it rang. Kelly dropped her folder, scattering animal pictures over the floor, and dashed for the phone. "Please let it be Joe," she muttered. All she needed was someone selling aluminum siding or magazine subscriptions or—

"Hello."

"Hello, Kelly." This time the caller was Nancy.

Kelly grimaced. She'd rather deal with Joe. "How are you?"

"We're fine, just a little concerned about Sean." Her voice betrayed no worry; it was as smooth as the woman herself. Kelly imagined her tossing her hair over her shoulder as she spoke.

"I explained the reason for this regression to Joe," Kelly said. "I don't want to see it get worse. He needs to be in familiar surroundings.'' Kelly hoped she sounded professional. She *felt* desperate.

''Don't you think he'll settle down soon and become accustomed to his new home?''

''I don't know, and I wouldn't recommend you take a chance.''

She heard Nancy say something to Joe, but she couldn't make out the words. Then Joe came on the line. ''All right. We'll consider bringing him back provided a few conditions are met.''

Oh, God, thank you. Now help me bring this off. ''I can't make deals for you. Why don't you call Sam Eldridge? I'm sure he can work out the arrangements.'' She gave Joe the number and couldn't help asking, ''Are . . . are you going to call?''

''Yes.''

''I'm glad. Give Sean a hug for me, would you?''

When she put the receiver down, Kelly's hands were shaking and she was dripping with sweat. She sat back in the chair and shut her eyes.

When Sam called half an hour later to tell her the Hamiltons were in Albuquerque and he'd arranged for Grant to pick up Sean, she didn't even try to hide her feelings. Tears ran down her cheeks, and she knew they were in her voice as well. ''Oh, Sam. I'm so thankful you could work things out.''

''You deserve the thanks. You handled the Hamiltons beautifully.''

Kelly laughed through her tears. ''Let's not worry about thanking anyone. The important thing is, Sean's coming home.''

Grant watched the ground come closer as the plane descended toward the Albuquerque airport. A few more minutes and he'd see his son. ''Thank God,'' he whispered as he had over and over in the last twenty-four hours.

He'd gone numb when Sam had called and said, "We've found him."

With all the effort he could muster, he'd kept his voice from breaking when he asked, "Where? Is he all right?"

"He's in New Mexico, and he's fine. Actually, he has a slight problem—"

"I thought you said he was all right. Is he sick? Has he had an accident?"

"No, no. He's cut down on his talking, that's all. Joe and Nancy spoke to Kelly—"

"To Kelly?" Grant roared. "Was she in on the kidnapping then?" He'd berated himself every minute for what he'd done to Kelly and sworn when this was over, he'd go to her and apologize. Now Sam was telling him she'd been involved all along.

"Calm down, Stuart. The only way she's 'in on' this is that Joe called her because he was worried about Sean. They wanted her to come out and work with him, get him talking again. Kelly convinced them to let him come back. You owe her, pal."

"God, yes," Grant had murmured with relief and promised himself he'd make it up to her.

Now he felt the bump as the plane's wheels touched the ground, and he unbuckled his seat belt. He was in the aisle and heading for the door before the FASTEN SEAT BELT sign went off, earning himself a disapproving glare from the flight attendant, but he didn't care.

He sprinted through the terminal and hailed a cab. When they pulled up before a white adobe cottage, he told the driver to wait, then strode up the sidewalk. Before he reached the door, it opened and Joe came outside. "Grant," he said, putting out his hand and barring the way inside.

Grant frowned at his former father-in-law. Was he up to some kind of trick? *Not here*, he thought. *Not now*. He'd gone through too much, come too damn far to put up with any last-minute schemes. He ignored

Joe's outstretched hand and stared at him coolly. "Where's Sean?"

"Nancy's getting him ready. He's fine. I believe you brought some papers."

Grant reached into his jacket pocket. "Yes, there'll be no prosecution for the—" He wanted to call it by its name, "kidnapping," but he substituted the terminology Joe preferred. "—for the unscheduled visit with you."

He handed Joe the papers, watched him peruse them, then nod and sign. Grant let out a breath. The worst was over.

"I'll tell Nancy you're ready to go," Joe said.

In a minute Nancy came out, holding Sean by the hand. The child's eyes widened when he saw Grant. "Daddy," he shouted, dropping his grandmother's hand and running toward Grant.

Grant took two steps forward, and they met. He bent and lifted Sean into his arms, holding him tight, not bothering to disguise the tears that moistened his cheeks. "Sean," he said hoarsely, "I've missed you, son."

"Can we go home now?"

"Yes," Grant said. "We can go home." Over Sean's shoulder, he looked at Joe and Nancy. They, too, had tears in their eyes, and Grant realized that Kelly had been partially right. Though they might be self-centered and demanding, they loved Sean, too.

He stepped forward. "I assume you'll want this Christmas with Sean." He saw the looks of surprise on both their faces and added, "I don't see any reason to deny you access to Sean, provided you abide by the rules the court set down."

"Thank you," Joe said softly.

Grant put Sean down. "Go tell Grandmother and Granddad good-bye, son. You'll see them again soon."

Joe bent to kiss the child, and Nancy knelt down and

took him in her arms. "Be a good boy, darling. We'll miss you."

Sean apparently had enough kissing. He turned, picked up the teddy bear he'd dropped when he'd seen his father, and peered up at Grant. "We going on the plane now?"

"In a little while."

Satisfied, Sean nodded. "I wanna sit by the window."

Grant took his hand and they started toward the cab. "Fine with me."

"I want peanuts and soda."

He'd better set some limits, or the kid would have him wound around his little finger. "We'll share."

Sean cocked his head and considered this for a moment, then climbed into the cab. "Okay, I'll share with you."

The cab pulled away from the curb, and Sean sat quietly, clutching his bear. Grant kept his arm around the child, taking in the softness of Sean's hair, the sweetness of his little-boy scent. He reveled in the wonder of hearing his child's voice again after he'd almost given up hope. He glanced out at the grandeur of the mountains, at the starkness of the desert, and marveled at their beauty, but then in his happiness at having Sean beside him, he found everything beautiful.

Sean began to cry.

Grant frowned. "What's wrong, son? Did you leave something at Granddad's?"

"Huh-uh." The child shook his head.

"Do you hurt somewhere? Do you have a tummy ache?"

Again Sean shook his head but cried all the harder.

"Tell me, Sean. Do you want something?"

The boy nodded but continued to sob. Grant got a handkerchief from his pocket and tried to wipe Sean's nose. The child shook his head vigorously and pushed Grant's hand away.

"Look, Sean. You have to tell me what you want, or I can't help you."

The sobs dissipated but loud hiccups followed. At last Sean whimpered, "Where's Kelly? Why she not come? I want Kelly."

Grant stared down into his son's tear-stained face. Where indeed was Kelly? She belonged here, with them. The three of them were a family. "School starts tomorrow. We'll see her then," he assured Sean. "I want Kelly, too."

The bell rang and children spilled from classrooms into the hall, shoving one another and chattering. Kelly stood at her doorway and watched, enjoying the first day of school excitement. She was glad of the uproar, the clamoring voices, the demands of time schedules and lesson plans. More than anything, she needed her work to occupy her time and distract her thoughts.

She'd endured some arch looks and a couple of pointed questions from her colleagues, and a few parents had eyed her curiously—after all, she'd given them plenty to talk about this summer, with her name on the front pages for several days. But she'd taken that in stride, fending off comments and ignoring stares.

Sean was back at school, Marla had told her, but Kelly avoided the classroom of the older three-year-olds. She wasn't sure she could manage a reunion with him without breaking into tears.

She went outside, waved to a couple of kids as she crossed the parking lot, then got into her car and headed for home. On the way she stopped to pick up a few groceries for herself and some kitty treats for Walter. Lately, he'd relented a bit and had even begun purring when she stroked him.

At her condo, she shouldered the two grocery sacks, her purse, and her briefcase and, unable to see over the bags, negotiated the stairs with care.

"Let me carry those for you," a familiar voice said as she reached her apartment.

Kelly nearly dropped her parcels. "Grant!"

He took the bags from her arms, which had suddenly gone limp, then waited as she fumbled with her keys. "May I come in?"

"Yes," she whispered, hoping he heard her answer but not her thudding heart.

She followed him, wondering what to do, what to say as he carried her groceries into the kitchen and deposited them on the counter. They returned to the living room, where Kelly sank onto the couch. She stared at Grant as if he were an apparition. Why was he here?

He sat down across from her and leaned forward, hands on his knees. "I need to talk to you."

"Okay." So much for communication. She couldn't seem to get out more than one word at a time. She cleared her throat and managed to ask, "How's Sean?"

"None the worse for his experience."

"Is he talking again?"

Grant chuckled. "Nonstop." His laughter died and he looked at her with an intensity that made her uncomfortable, uncertain. "I want to thank you for what you did."

She shrugged it off, feeling even more uncomfortable now. "I didn't do anything. Joe called me."

"But you convinced him Sean belonged here. I can't thank you enough."

For a horrible moment, she feared Grant might offer her some type of reward, perhaps another check for her school, but seconds passed and he did nothing but look at her seriously. Then he spoke, "I owe you an apology."

"No."

"I do. We both know that. I said some terrible things last week and I—"

"Please, Grant. Just leave it." She didn't want to

rehash what had happened. He'd voiced his thanks and his apology, and she wanted him to go away—before she embarrassed them both by throwing herself into his arms.

She started to rise, to let him know their discussion was over, but he shook his head. "Let me finish, please. You'd given me every reason to trust you and none to doubt you. I know it's no excuse, but in the turmoil of losing Sean, Claudia and her duplicity kept popping into my mind and somehow I got the two of you confused. And there was the money. None of what I conjured up about that made any sense. I knew I was dead wrong as soon as I said the words, but it was too late."

"It's over now." She saw him take a long breath as if he'd been released from a burden, then went on. "I've thought a lot about the money and what I should do with it. I almost returned it to Joe and Nancy." She saw he was ready to protest that and shook her head. "I didn't. I want to believe . . I *do* believe they gave that money with no strings attached. I'm going to use it for my school, so children like Sean will benefit."

"I'm glad," Grant said, surprising her. "Something good will come of this after all."

"Well," Kelly said with a brightness she didn't feel, "I'm glad we agree. Thanks for coming by." She stood up.

"Please sit down."

Gray eyes stared at her earnestly, and she complied. Why wouldn't he leave? Why did he have to sit here, so close she could almost touch him, so near she could smell his after-shave? Too close. Too near. Her fingers itched to stroke his cheek; her body ached to press against him. She closed her eyes to shut out the vision of dark curling hair, twilight gray eyes, and a mouth made to fuse with hers. When she opened them, she said as lightly as she could, "Do you have something else to talk about?"

"Several things. The first is Sean."

"I thought you said he was doing well."

"He is, but he needs you, Kelly."

"Not anymore." She walked away to stare out the window. She couldn't face a discussion of Sean, couldn't face Grant. "I already told you I planned to dismiss him. We'll have an official discharge conference next week if that's convenient for you. I intended to have the school secretary call; but since you're here, we'll schedule it now."

"Schedule the conference whenever you like. I'll be there." His voice came closer, until she could feel him standing directly behind her. Kelly tensed. "I don't care if you drop him from your caseload, but I don't want you to drop out of his life."

He put his hands on her shoulders and turned her to face him. His face was very close, his eyes dark and serious. Kelly trembled. "I want you to come back, Kelly. I need you, too."

"Grant—" she whispered weakly.

"There hasn't been a night since you left that I haven't wakened wanting you. Come home with me."

She watched, mesmerized, as his head lowered. His lips were scant inches from hers when his words registered in her mind. "No!" She shoved at his chest and pushed past him. She strode across the room, then swung around to face him, hands on her hips. "No!" she repeated. "I've already sacrificed my reputation for you in the courtroom, but that was necessary. But this—forget it. I won't be your live-in lover."

He spread his hands and walked to her purposefully. She refused to give way. "I mean it, Grant."

He drew a breath. "Have I miscommunicated my intentions so thoroughly? Like my son, I'm a man of few words. I wasn't asking you to live with me. I want you to marry me." Kelly gasped and he continued. "I realized when I brought Sean home that we were meant to be a family. I love you . . . and I trust you."

"Oh, Grant," she whispered, going into his arms. "I love you, too."

He kissed her with all the pent-up longing of a week of separation, and she reveled in the feel of him, the knowledge of his love. "When?" he asked as he tore his lips away. "When can we get married?"

Giddy with joy, she answered, "Tomorrow. Next week. As soon as I can arrange a few days off. You promised me an island vacation, remember? We could make it a honeymoon."

Grant drew back and gave her a sheepish grin. "Ah, about that trip. I was thinking about a, ah, family honeymoon. Maybe to Disney World."

Kelly laughed. "Sounds fine to me."

He drew her back into his arms. "I love you. I know I'm not the world's best communicator, so remind me to tell you that every day."

She smiled up at him, took his hand, and led him into her bedroom. "I will, but sometimes, my love, it's better to show than tell."

SHARE THE FUN . . .
SHARE YOUR NEW-FOUND TREASURE!!

You don't want to let your new books out of your sight? That's okay. Your friends can get their own. Order below.

No. 153 A MAN OF FEW WORDS by Thelma Zirkelbach
Kelly *never* mixes business with pleasure! Why is Grant the exception?

No. 59 13 DAYS OF LUCK by Lacey Dancer
Author Pippa Weldon finds her real-life hero in Joshua Luck.

No. 60 SARA'S ANGEL by Sharon Sala
Sara *must* get to Hawk. He's the only one who can help.

No. 61 HOME FIELD ADVANTAGE by Janice Bartlett
Marian shows John there is more to life than just professional sports.

No. 62 FOR SERVICES RENDERED by Ann Patrick
Nick's life is in perfect order until he meets Claire!

No. 63 WHERE THERE'S A WILL by Leanne Banks
Chelsea goes toe-to-toe with her new, unhappy business partner.

No. 64 YESTERDAY'S FANTASY by Pamela Macaluso
Melissa always had a crush on Morgan. Maybe dreams do come true!

No. 65 TO CATCH A LORELEI by Phyllis Houseman
Lorelei sets a trap for Daniel but gets caught in it herself.

No. 66 BACK OF BEYOND by Shirley Faye
Dani and Jesse are forced to face their true feelings for each other.

No. 67 CRYSTAL CLEAR by Cay David
Max could be the end of all Chrystal's dreams . . . or just the beginning!

No. 68 PROMISE OF PARADISE by Karen Lawton Barrett
Gabriel is surprised to find that Eden's beauty is not just skin deep.

No. 69 OCEAN OF DREAMS by Patricia Hagan
Is Jenny just another shipboard romance to Officer Kirk Moen?

No. 70 SUNDAY KIND OF LOVE by Lois Faye Dyer
Trace literally sweeps beautiful, ebony-haired Lily off her feet.

No. 71 ISLAND SECRETS by Darcy Rice
Chad has the power to take away Tucker's hard-earned independence.

No. 72 COMING HOME by Janis Reams Hudson
Clint always loved Lacey. Now Fate has given them another chance.

No. 73 KING'S RANSOM by Sharon Sala
Jesse was always like King's little sister. When did it all change?

No. 74 **A MAN WORTH LOVING** by Karen Rose Smith
Nate's middle name is 'freedom' . . . that is, until Shara comes along.

No. 75 **RAINBOWS & LOVE SONGS** by Catherine Sellers
Dan has more than one problem. One of them is named Kacy!

No. 76 **ALWAYS ANNIE** by Patty Copeland
Annie is down-to-earth and real . . . and Ted's never met anyone like her.

No. 77 **FLI~~GHT~~** ~~SOLD OUT~~ Lacey Dancer
Rich had decid~~e~~ ....~~nce for~~ good until Christiana.

No. 78 **TO LOVE A COWBOY** by Laura Phillips
Dee is the dark-haired beauty that sends Nick reeling back to the past.

No. 79 **SASSY LADY** by Becky Barker
No matter how hard he tries, Curt can't seem to get away from Maggie.

No. 80 **CRITIC'S CHOICE** by Kathleen Yapp
Marlis can't do one thing right in front of her handsome houseguest.

No. 81 **TUNE IN TOMORROW** by Laura Michaels
Deke happily gave up life in the fast lane. Can Liz do the same?

Meteor Publishing Corporation
Dept. 693, P. O. Box 41820, Philadelphia, PA 19101-9828

Please send the books I've indicated below. Check or money order (U.S. Dollars only)—no cash, stamps or C.O.D.s (PA residents, add 6% sales tax). I am enclosing $2.95 plus 75¢ handling fee for *each* book ordered.

Total Amount Enclosed: $_____.

___ No. 153	___ No. 64	___ No. 70	___ No. 76
___ No. 59	___ No. 65	___ No. 71	___ No. 7~~7~~
___ No. 60	___ No. 66	___ No. 72	___ No. 78
___ No. 61	___ No. 67	___ No. 73	___ No. 79
___ No. 62	___ No. 68	___ No. 74	___ No. 80
___ No. 63	___ No. 69	___ No. 75	___ No. 81

Please Print:
Name _____
Address _____ Apt. No. _____
City/State _____ Zip _____

Allow four to six weeks for delivery. Quantities limited.